CHRISTMAS STORIES FOR KIDS 8-12

12 SHORT STORIES ABOUT THE MAGIC OF CHRISTMAS

BERNARD TATE

TOMOKAI RIVER

Illustrations by Maria Solias

CONTENTS

GET YOUR KIDS READY FOR CHRISTMAS!

Download this free, ready-to-print Letter to Santa, *and* get signed up to receive more free offers from Tomokai River Publishing (like free kid's books).

Scan the QR code with your phone!

1

THE MAGIC POND

Max was three steps ahead of his friends as they charged towards the pond in the nearby park. They had all been fidgeting since dinner, desperate to get on the ice and practice their skating moves. After endless gray days, the sun had finally broken through the clouds that morning and Max hoped Theo, who was an ace at video recording on his phone, would capture him performing a triple spin. *That* would make him the talk of his class when school started up again after the Christmas break.

When the adolescent friends finally skidded to a stop at the edge of the frozen pond, Max was first to rip his sneakers off and tug his skates from his rucksack. He barely noticed that the others were standing stock still until he stood up himself, balancing on his blades in the soft mud.

"What's up, you guys? Aren't you coming on? Look, the ice is so smooth!" he exclaimed excitedly as he tapped the ice with the edge of his blade, then slowly pushed off and glided to the center of the pond.

"Um, Max? There are a few more puddles on there than there were yesterday," Theo warned nervously.

"Yeah Max, the sun is kinda warmer than we thought," Chase's eyes were glued to the tree hanging over the mouth of the pond, rhythmically dripping raindrops onto the ice.

"You bunch of wimps!" Max spun around in a perfect circle and jerked to a stop, stomping his heel into the ice to show just how solid it was. But suddenly, a faint cracking sound, like an egg falling to a kitchen floor, startled the group and pulled their eyes to the space beneath Max's feet. A jagged lightning bolt shape flew across the frozen ice, which then gave way, plunging Max into the bitterly cold water below.

Max windmilled his arms furiously as he disappeared into the dark water, kicking his skated feet with all his might toward the surface. As he did, he squinted up at the hole he had fallen through, trying to figure out if he was getting closer to it or farther away. Then, everything went black.

Max furiously coughed into the slushy, dazzling white ground, which jolted him awake. He gulped in air, but instead inhaled a mouthful of powdered snow. He spat it back out in a cloud. He looked around, confused. Where were his friends? Where was the park? He spun around onto his butt to see the same familiar pond where they'd always hung out, and the shattered ice floating on the water's surface like panes of glass. But everything around it was an unfamiliar winter wonderland.

Snow stretched in every direction, as far as the eye could see. His neighborhood had vanished, and all he could make out around him were hills and plains of fluffy white drifts. He gazed in astonishment, and was only distracted when a shudder ran through his body that made him feel like he was sitting on top of a spinning washing machine. He was *freezing!*

He wrapped his arms tightly around his body and felt his soaking wet clothes beginning to harden with ice. He hadn't paid much attention in Boy Scouts when they'd covered survival in the wild (he was far too busy working on breaking the world record for 'Biggest Gum Wad of all Time', and that had taken some seriously concentrated chewing), but he knew if he didn't get warm soon, things wouldn't end too well for him because he'd be a Maxcicle.

Suddenly, he heard a faint noise behind him. He turned to see what it was, but all he saw was a large hill of snow. He strained his ears and again heard a sound. He was almost sure it was a tiny cough.

"Hey, who's there?" he called nervously. He listened once more, and then, a small *achoo!* floated through the air. Max scrambled to his feet.

"You better come out or… or…" he tried to remember what a tough guy would say in such a situation. He definitely wasn't a tough guy, but he was pretty sure acting the part would save his skin for at least a *few* seconds while he ran in the opposite direction from the noise like he was being chased by a wildebeest.

"I do apologize," squeaked a tiny voice from somewhere in the snow. Max crept slowly forward, then a surge of courage caused him to take two huge leaps to see who was hiding behind the hill. To his astonishment, a miniature man, no higher than Max's hip, stood sheepishly holding a folded blanket beside a pair of red skis. He wore the most unusual outfit; green velvet pants with suspenders peeking out from behind his matching green jacket. Golden buttons dotted each side of the jacket, and he wore a bright red shirt, so bright, in fact, it almost had the effect of making his cheeks look even ruddier. His cone-shaped hat was a shimmering emerald color and stuck up from his head like a miniature wonky tree. He looked bashfully up at Max and offered him the blanket.

"This should take the chill out, for now," he said, his voice barely a whisper. When Max took the blanket from him, the little man quickly shoved his hands into his pockets, burrowing his face as best he could into the oversized bowtie around his neck.

"We really must hurry, things are running ahead of schedule at the workshop," the man said shyly, looking at the ground. "If we are to get you home, we must get you into the sleigh before anyone sees you."

"The what?" Max asked, quickly unfolding the blanket and throwing it around his shoulders. It was strangely warm, as if it had been plugged into a socket and heated up.

"The sleigh. We'll hide you under the sack. It worked a few years ago, when another child fell through the pond just as you did."

"You'll hide me under the *what?* Someone *fell through* the pond?" Max decided his ears must be filled with water. And perhaps he'd hit his head. And there was definitely something wrong with his eyes, because the fellow in front of him looked like he'd been through three rounds inside a laundry machine.

"Please put this on," the small man said, holding out a hat just like his own. Max took it between his finger and thumb and inspected it as if it was a rotten-smelling sock. The man sighed impatiently at Max's confused face.

"You'll need to kneel on these skis too. Pull the blanket tight around you, so no one can see your body. Gosh, you human children seem to get bigger and bigger every year!"

Max was absolutely baffled. But instead of asking any more questions, he did as he was told, and squashed the hat onto his head before lowering himself onto the skis. He noticed they were attached to a length of rope, which the little man took hold of.

"Now what?" he asked.

"We just need to keep a low profile, that's all. We want to avoid anyone else seeing you. My folk get... well, very excited when they see human children," the man explained. He began to slowly pull the skis along the snow, huffing and puffing as he moved. Max felt like a sack of potatoes.

After a couple of minutes, the snow became a little icier, and Max sensed the earth had tipped slightly downward. The man balled the rope up in his hands and jumped onto the skis in front of Max as they began to slide down a snowy hill.

"What's your name? Where are we?" Max yelled, as the tip of the man's hat prodded him in the nose. He saw some buildings begin to take shape at the foot of the hill, growing larger and larger as they gained speed. A giant red barn appeared, with strange pink, glittering smoke chugging from its chimney. What looked like horses with unusual, stick-shaped bridles on their heads peered out from a row of open stable doors. Christmas music drifted out of a bakery that looked very much like a gingerbread house. The distant calls of tinny voices and whistles drifted through Max's eardrums.

"My name is Freddy, and never you mind where we are. All you need to know is that it is far, far away from your home, which I will be promptly be returning you to," he replied, sounding a little annoyed.

"Freddy, just out of curiosity," Max shouted as the wind whipped at their cheeks. The skis were really moving now! "Are you... an elf?"

"I am *elvin!*" Freddy scoffed, leaning back to slow their skis as they maneuvered into town. Max stared with wonder. Hundreds of tiny people just like Freddy were scurrying to and fro, their arms piled high with wrapping paper, ribbons, boxes and toys. He was so amazed he almost leapt up from the skis.

"Don't you dare!" scolded Freddy, clamping his tiny hands to the hem of the blanket, bolting Max in place. "You have no idea what a frenzy you'll cause if they realize you're here."

"But this is like a dream. I need to see for myself if it's real!" Max countered. He hadn't noticed that the skis continued to move, even though the ground they were on was completely flat. Freddy steered them down an alleyway to the left, where a huge garage door loomed. Freddy snapped his fingers, and as they approached, the door began to slide upwards. A gigantic, ruby red vehicle was slowly unveiled, sparkling in the sunlight. It was trimmed with white fur, much, Max presumed, like the man who drove it.

"Am I going to meet Santa?!" Max gasped with glee, as the skis slowed to a stop just inside the garage. He uncoiled his legs and threw the blanket off his shoulders.

Freddy hurried to the door of the sleigh and pulled it open. He gestured to Max to climb in. "No, you won't meet him. He mustn't know you're here. We can't have him distracted on the most important night of the year. You'll be safe under the sack. Here, I'll even throw in some snacks from the Candy Corner Store," Freddy offered.

Max didn't need to be told twice. He gripped the glittering side of the sleigh and jumped in, nestling himself among the mounds of materials draped behind the seats. "Won't the toys crush me when the elves start filling the sack?" he asked, burrowing underneath until he was almost invisible.

"Not at all. The sack is magical," said Freddy proudly. "It is always light as a feather. Now, the sleigh will let you know when you have arrived at your house. I'd recommend taking a nap for the first few hours while the Big Man loops around Europe. Or else you could enjoy the Christmas lights."

The somewhat grumpy elf suddenly smiled kindly, and shut the door, putting his finger to his lips to remind Max to remain quiet. Max whispered his thanks, and squeezed his eyes shut as he waited for take-off. He must have drifted off to sleep, because he dreamed of starry skies, a whirl of jewelled colors, and a large, bearded man winking down at him from above.

Max's alarm blasted him awake and he instinctively reached over and smacked it off, just as he did every morning. He opened his eyes sleepily and looked around his room. He could hear his little sister running up and down the hallway, screeching that Santa had been there. He marvelled at how real his dream had seemed. It was as if he really had been to the North Pole.

Disappointment washed over him as he stood up and stretched. But then something fell off his head and landed at his feet. It was an emerald, cone-shaped hat! Max gasped. *Was it possible?* he wondered.

2

THE LITTLE LOST PRESENT

It was Christmas morning and the house was silent and still. The cookies had been eaten. The milk had been drunk. Stockings were brimming with candy and presents and all sorts of other good things. Santa Claus had come and gone, and a beautiful pile of brightly wrapped presents sat under the tree that had been decorated with colorful ornaments and lights, each gift just waiting to be opened.

But there was one present — a very special present — tucked way back under the tree that Santa had saved for the most special child of all.

It was just a little square box, but it was wrapped in pretty paper with a lovely bow. The little present knew it wasn't the shiniest or biggest gift under the tree, but it was a gift that any child would love. The little present had an important job to do, so it waited under the soft glow of the tree as Christmas Eve turned into Christmas morning, hoping it would be found and enjoyed.

Before the sun rose, the children raced from their beds in their new candy cane and gingerbread pajamas. Their thoughts were filled with sweet dreams as they rubbed their eyes and stood before the tree. They giggled and gasped as they saw all the wonderful gifts that Santa had left for them; basketballs and skateboards, pretty dolls and all kinds of other toys. There were so many gifts, the children didn't know where to begin!

"Can we open our presents now?" the boy excitedly asked his parents.

"Please? Oh, look what Santa brought!" exclaimed his sister.

"Yes, but wait your turn," Dad said patiently, and covered his mouth with a yawn.

"You must have been good this year," Mom observed. "Santa left so many presents!"

The little present tucked way back behind the tree shivered with excitement as the family settled in and began to pass the gifts around. The little present had waited all year long, hoping for this very moment. Who would open it? Would the children like what was inside? Would they be excited? Christmas music played softly as each child opened their presents one by one.

"I got a rocket ship!" exclaimed the little boy.

"I got a pony!" said the little girl, holding up her new toy pony.

And with each gift that was opened, the little present tucked behind the tree became more and more excited. It was the greatest honor to become a Christmas present, chosen specially by Santa for a very special child. The little present knew that whichever child was lucky enough to open it would be filled with wonder and joy. The little present could barely contain its excitement as the children tore through wrapping paper, boxes, bags and bows until it was the only gift left under the tree.

The little boy searched at the back of the tree. "There's nothing else left!"

"Looks like you've opened all the gifts," Dad said.

"Let's go have breakfast," Mom said.

"Okay!" The children rose from their Christmas treasures and followed their parents to the kitchen. The little present was lost.

Wait! Don't go! The little present could barely contain its tears. Will anyone open me this Christmas?

The little lost present began to grow worried. Santa had hidden it too well! What if they forgot all about it? What if it was accidentally thrown away? What if the good little children never got to open up Santa's most special present of all? The thought made the little present so sad it wanted to cry. Would the children find it and open their littlest gift before Christmas was over?

All that day, the little present sat hidden as the children played with their toys and helped their parents prepare for Christmas dinner. Family came to visit and delicious smells filled the air as they enjoyed their holiday meal. There was singing and laughing and Christmas songs and movies. So many people passed by, but no one noticed the pretty little forgotten present hidden away at the back of the tree.

The little present tried to be patient, tried to cheer up. It wasn't as though Santa meant for the most important present of all to become lost! But as the sun began to set and a chill filled the air, the little present began to lose hope. The little gift sang itself a sad Christmas song to pass the time.

I'm just a little lost present
Tucked in the back of the tree
Just a sad little lonely lost present
Oh, won't someone please open me?

All I wanted this Christmas
Was to bring lots of joy
To a sweet little girl
Or a kind little boy.

But now I am stuck
Lost under the tree skirt.
Someone even stepped on me!
And, ouch, did it hurt!

It makes me so sad
That no one can see
A lost little present
Like little old me.

I've waited all year
For this one special day
To make someone smile
To be happy and play.

My paper is pretty
My bow is so shiny
I promise big fun
Even though I am tiny.

What's inside? A surprise!
But I bet you can guess
It isn't new socks
Or a new party dress.

Santa chose me specially
As a fun little treat.
I'm not something you wear
Or something you eat.

But here I still sit,
All alone and forgotten.
It's such a sad shame.
Oh, I just feel so rotten!

Just then, the little lost present felt a small, warm hand wrap around its box. All at once it was lifted up, up, up and away from under the tree. A sweet little girl stared down at the present, her eyes sparkling and full of wonder.

What's that? Oh my stars!

Oh my sugarplum cake!
Did someone just find me?
Oh, yes, for goodness sake!

"Mommy! There's one more present! It was lost under the tree!" The little girl leaned in and whispered, "Oh, I wish it was for me."

"It must be for you," her mom said with a smile. "Go ahead, open it. It's been back there a while."

It's a Christmas miracle!
A holiday dream come true!
They found me! Hooray!
But now... what do I do?

I'll stay still and so calm
And I'll try not to quiver.
As they open my lid
I won't let out a shiver.

A child of my own!
What a wonderful thing!
I hope that they like me!
Oh it makes my heart sing!

The little girl smiled as she opened the lid to the little lost present. She stared at the box for almost a minute, trying to figure out just what was in it. She finally picked up the treasure and held it in her hand; it was a small snowflake, no bigger than a grain of sand. Inside the box was a note signed from Santa himself, a letter of explanation from the North Pole's head elf.

Merry Christmas!
I know you've been good
Please take care of this snowflake
Just as you should.

Hold tight to this Christmassy feeling
Of goodwill and cheer.
Tell everyone about Christmas!
Sing loud for all to hear!
Hold on to Christmas

And all you hold dear,
And I'm sure to visit again
If you're good next year.
— S. Claus

The little girl smiled, closed her eyes and did as Santa had said. She felt something warm grow inside her and felt happier and more full of good cheer than ever before. Everything sparkled around her and she was filled with the joy of Christmas. If she held tight, she could share that joy with others and learn to make it last all year long.

"I'll keep you safe," she whispered and carefully tucked the snowflake away in its box.

"What did you get?" Mom asked. "What was in the box?"

"Oh, nothing," the girl winked at the little lost present and yawned. "Time for bed."

The girl held the little lost present to her chest and they went off to bed, with dreams of next Christmas already dancing in her head. She placed the gift next to her bed and kissed it goodnight, where she would keep it until next year. Yes, the holiday was over, but the true meaning of Christmas would always be in her heart as long as she believed.

The little lost present wasn't lost anymore, and as Christmas day ended, the special little gift felt so much happiness. Even though the children had received so many wonderful toys that year, the little present knew that it was the greatest gift of all. The spirit of Christmas is so small you can barely see it, and sometimes it's easy to lose. But if you hold on tight and if you believe, maybe Santa will leave a little lost present for you to find next Christmas Eve!

3

LOST ON CHRISTMAS EVE

It was the afternoon before Christmas, and the North Pole was in crisis. Everywhere you looked, elves were running to and fro, trying to prepare everything in time for Santa Claus to depart on his sleigh. They only had a few hours, and they were behind schedule. This didn't usually happen, of course. Santa and his elves spent all year planning and preparing for this very day. But this year, they had been particularly unlucky.

In early November, they had been bombarded by the heaviest snowfall they'd seen in decades. It had piled up ten feet high on the roof of the workshop, which caused the whole thing to cave in overnight. The devastated elves dug through the wreckage to find that most of the toys stored there had been completely crushed, and they would need to start making them all over again.

Everyone was working extra hard to make sure the presents were ready in time, including Santa himself. Normally he would be triple-checking his list right now, but instead he was helping tie ribbons on the last few presents to be wrapped.

Over at the stables, the reindeer could feel the tension in the air as everyone rushed around. They would've been happy to help wrap presents as well, but unfortunately their hooves weren't nimble enough. So instead they were doing what they could to prepare for the worst—if the presents weren't finished in time, Santa would be late, which would mean the reindeer would have to fly faster than they'd ever flown before to make sure he still got to all the houses before Christmas morning. They had been running drills and practicing as much as possible to ensure they were ready for the big day. Even as they stood waiting to be buckled into their harnesses, they were stretching their legs and rolling their shoulders so they'd be ready to go at a moment's notice.

Normally, a small team of trained elves were in charge of preparing the reindeer and the sleigh for take-off. But since most everyone was working on the presents this afternoon, only the sleigh manager, Snowball, and his apprentice, Rosemary, were in the stable. Snowball was busy checking over the sleigh and supervising the presents as they were loaded in, and Rosemary was focusing on the reindeer. There were a lot of buckles and bells to be secured. Rosemary had practiced doing this many times before, so she was pretty confident that she was doing everything correctly.

"How's it going over there?" Snowball called to her while she was securing Donner's harness.

"Almost done!" Rosemary called back, giving her supervisor a thumbs up before moving on to Blitzen's harness.

With only minutes to go before he had to take off, Santa climbed into his sleigh. Normally he would give a speech thanking the elves for all their hard work, but there simply wasn't the time.

"Excellent job everyone," he said with a broad smile. "We'll celebrate when I return in the morning!"

He grabbed the reins, and they were off, in the nick of time. It was a stormy, cloudy night. If Rudolph wasn't leading to light the way, there was no way Santa would have been able to see where he was going.

As they drew near to the first village, Santa directed the reindeer downward through the clouds. They made a sharp descent, an easy maneuver that the reindeers practiced all the time. But to Donner, this time felt different. He felt himself starting to wobble, and then he heard a *snap!*

Suddenly he was flying alone, but watched as the other eight reindeer continued to descend and then disappear into the clouds. He turned with alarm to see that a part of his harness was hanging loose. He realized it must not have been secured properly during all the chaos!

The clouds were so thick that Donner couldn't see the sleigh or even Rudolph's nose anywhere. He knew he needed to catch up to them quickly. All nine reindeer were essential, especially this year, since the sleigh would fly too slow without him. He raced downward in the direction they had been going. Donner would feel awful if even one child didn't receive their Christmas presents on time because of him.

He flew as quickly as he could, with the harsh, cold wind stinging his nose. If the clouds weren't so thick, he would be able to recognize their usual route and catch up to the sleigh in the nearest village. But without being able to spot any of the landmarks he was used to, he had no idea if he was going the right way.

This thought worried him, and he slowed down. He knew that Santa would make a few turns here and there to take advantage of the winds, and he probably wasn't following the right route. And if he got turned around and went too far in the wrong direction, he might never catch up!

He decided that the best option was to fly low, beneath the thickest clouds and fog. That way he could follow the route he was used to by watching the trees. When the fog began to clear as he flew lower, he realized that he was already below the tree tops. All around him were snow-covered trees, many decorated with lights and tinsel. It was beautiful, but Donner still had no idea where he was! He was used to seeing the trees from up above, so this did him no good at all.

Suddenly, there was a scuffling noise behind him, and he turned to see a white arctic rabbit hopping through the snow on the ground. "Excuse me!" Donner called as he flew down to talk to the rabbit. "I'm lost. Could you please point me in the direction of the nearest village?"

"I'm sorry, but I don't know which direction it is," the rabbit said apologetically. "We rabbits like to stay close to home, so I've never been to the village. But you're welcome to come inside and warm up for a while," offered the rabbit.

The rabbit hopped over to the entrance of a burrow at the base of a tree. A warm yellow light was emanating from it, and Donner could see that the rabbit's whole family was inside having their dinner. He could also see that the entrance was barely big enough for his nose to fit through. Even if he had the time to spare, he'd never fit.

"It looks quite cozy," said Donner appreciatively. "But I've really got to catch up with my sleigh. Thank you anyway."

"Good luck!" the rabbit called after him, and hopped into the burrow.

Donner knew he needed a new plan. Since flying low hadn't worked, he decided to do the opposite, and fly high up above the clouds. It took him a little while to get up there, but eventually he emerged from the storm clouds into a clear, black and blue night sky. The moon was shining and illuminating the tops of the swirling clouds, and if Donner weren't in such a hurry, he would have liked to spend some time stargazing up there. But there was no time for that. He searched the sky for the North Star, which was brighter than all the others and would help guide him. When he found it, he could look around for familiar constellations, and then follow them. He knew that the village was south of the North Pole, so maybe if he kept going south, he would get there.

It wasn't long before he saw something glowing below the clouds. He must have been closer to the village than he'd thought! He headed straight for the light, diving headfirst into the clouds.

CLUNK!

He'd run into something hard. He backed up, feeling dizzy, and shook his head to clear his vision. A glowing red light came into view, and it was attached to the face of Rudolph!

"Donner, I found you!" Rudolph yelled with delight. "We were so worried!"

"Thank goodness!" exclaimed Donner. "I was scared I would never catch up," he said with a sigh of relief.

"The fog was so thick we didn't notice you weren't with us until we landed on the first rooftop," Rudolph explained. "Otherwise, we would have rushed back right away!"

Rudolph led Donner towards the village, and told him they'd realized what had happened when they saw the broken harness. They had all been terribly worried about whether Donner was okay, but Santa wasn't sure it was safe for any one of them to go looking for him, and he still needed to get quickly from house to house. Rudolph volunteered to go looking, since now that they were in the village, Santa could use the streetlights to help him navigate, at least for a little while. Rudolph had flown straight up and run right into Donner.

"You almost made it all the way here on your own!" Rudolph said, impressed.

"It's not easy being alone," Donner said. "I'll be glad to be back with the team."

The two reindeer soon saw the yellow lights of the village glowing in the distance. Once they were low enough, it was easy to spot the red sleigh on top of one of the houses. The whole team cheered when they saw Rudolph and Donner. Santa popped his head out of the chimney just as their hooves landed on the roof.

"Donner, my boy!" Santa greeted warmly. "We were worried sick about you." He patted Donner affectionately and gave him some treats from his pocket. Then he fixed Donner's harness and made sure it was extra secure.

"There we go," he said with a smile. "Poor Rosemary is going to feel terrible when she hears what happened. But it all worked out in the end." He winked, then climbed back into the sleigh and took the reins.

The team took off, and it felt so good to be all together again. As they left the little village and flew towards the next one, Donner thought about the hardships they had faced this Christmas season, and knew without a doubt that they could handle anything, as long as they all worked together. That's how they managed to get Santa to every home in time for Christmas that year, and made it back to the North Pole for their own Christmas celebration.

4

THE SANTA WAFFLE SPARKLE
SPECTACULAR

"Mom," six-year-old Penny asked, spinning on the stool at the kitchen counter. "Is it Christmas yet?"

"Almost," her mom said, reaching out with one hand to stop Penny from spinning, and continuing to mix frosting with the other. "It's Christmas *Eve*."

Holiday music spilled into the kitchen from the living room, where Penny's little sister was busy coloring in the Christmas cards they planned to give to their neighbors along with the Christmas cookies.

"Ugh, it's *still* only Christmas Eve?" Penny complained, kicking the cabinet to set herself spinning again. "It's been Christmas Eve for *hours!*" She wore her new fuzzy red Christmas footsie pajamas, which she'd put on the moment the sun went down, even though she wasn't the least bit sleepy.

"Why don't you go tell your sister it's time to decorate the cookies?" Mom suggested, keeping a wary eye on Penny's long hair that was flying close to the frosting as she twirled.

Penny jumped off the stool, and almost fell, the slick bottoms of her footsie pajamas slipping on the tile floor. Delighted with this new discovery, Penny 'skated' the rest of the way out of the kitchen and into the living room.

"Maddie!" Penny yelled, sliding until she hopped onto the living room rug. Maddie sat crisscross-applesauce at the coffee table, her homemade cards surrounded by crayons, markers, and Christmas stickers. A fire crackled in the fireplace, and the Christmas tree lights cast a warm glow in front of the dark window.

"You look so cozy!" Penny squealed, sitting next to her sister, and pulling an uncolored card toward her.

Being "cozy" was Penny's very favorite thing, especially when it was Christmas. She joined her sister in singing along with the music and coloring, until their mom called from the kitchen: "Are these cookies going to decorate themselves?"

The girls jumped up, and in their matching red fuzzy pjs, slid into the kitchen and took their seats on the stools in front of the counter.

This was the best part of Christmas, Penny thought, happily squirting green frosting all over a cookie Christmas tree before realizing it wasn't actually a tree. "I made a green angel!" she said happily, holding it up to show her mom, who gave a thumbs-up from where she sat with her feet up at the kitchen table, chatting on the phone with their Auntie Caroline.

It was hard work, decorating all these cookies for their neighbors. Purple Christmas trees, blue stockings, green angels, orange Santas and rainbow bells, Penny and Maddie made them all as they crooned along with the music. Their mom stuck a finger in the ear that wasn't pressed to the phone and went into the living room to continue talking.

That's when they discovered that the louder they sang, the better the cookies came out, and soon they were singing at the top of their lungs, adding tiny candies, gum drops and leftover zombie eyeballs from Halloween to their cookie creations.

Finally, the girls' work was done. Piled high on eight holiday plates along the counter were the most deco-rated cookies in the history of Christmas cookies.

"How'd it go?" their mom said, her eyes widening as she came back into the kitchen and took in their hard work.

Penny and Maddie beamed as their mom looked at their cookies, commenting on the creative color combinations, the abundance of frosting, and the use of zombie eyeballs. She carefully wrapped each plate and was just about to get the homemade cards from the living room when Penny screamed.

"SANTA!!" she wailed.

"WHERE?!" her sister and mom asked, both of them spinning around, even though only one was on a spinning stool.

"We forgot to make him cookies!" Penny cried, her voice cracking. "And we used up all the ingredients!"

"We don't have no more 'gredients!" her little sister echoed; her own voice dangerously close to crying. "Not even eyeballs," she moaned.

Their mom let out a big breath and sucked one just as big right back in. "Okay. That's okay," she reassured them, scanning the kitchen counters, which were very, very empty of leftover Christmas cookies. "We can just take one from each..." She started to unwrap a plate.

"Noooo!" the girls wailed in unison. "We have to make his SPECIAL!"

"Of course, you do," their mom agreed, opening the refrigerator door as if there might be an extra stack of cookies inside. The girls slid off their stools and stood on either side of their mom and peered into the fridge with her.

"We can give him the pumpkin pie," Penny suggested helpfully, because she hated pumpkin pie and if Santa ate it, it meant she wouldn't have to look at its weird squishy yuckiness at her grandma's tomorrow.

"We're not giving him the pumpkin pie," her mom scolded. "Hey, how about some French onion dip?"

"Santa likes *cookies*, Mom," Maddie explained. "Only cookies."

"Okay," their mom said, moving things around in the fridge. "Only cookies. Not leftover pizza? It's pepperoni."

"*Cookies*," the girls repeated forcefully, again in unison.

"Aha!" their mom exclaimed, moving them back so she could close the refrigerator door and pull open the freezer drawer. "It's not a cookie, but it's doughy and a little sweet and round like a cookie…" she said as she dug deep into the freezer, pulling out a giant freezer bag so frosty that they couldn't make out its contents. She opened the bag, slipped her hand inside and triumphantly pulled out...

"Toaster waffles?" Penny asked, her nose wrinkling with disgust.

"Toasty waffles!" Maddie screamed happily, "I love those!"

"I know it's not a cookie," their mom said gently, closing the freezer. "But I think you two will make it so beautiful, Santa will like it better than any other cookie he gets tonight." She smiled with confidence.

A while later, after the first toaster waffle had burned, and the second had accidentally been eaten by Maddie because she was hungry, the third and final toaster waffle was perfectly toasted and cooling on a paper plate on the counter. There was the tiniest bit of frosting left, a deep purple, which the girls carefully spread over every inch of the waffle.

"I wish there was more decorating stuff," Penny said sadly, looking at the purple circle.

"Yeah, we need some eatable glitter," Maddie suggested.

"Edible," their mom corrected, before breaking into a grin and opening the cabinet over the stove. "Liiiike... this?"

The sisters cheered when they saw the big jar of pink and purple sparkly cookie glitter their mom held up.

"IT'S A CHRISTMAS MIRACLE!" Penny shouted.

"Okay, you two get to decorating," their mom said. "I'm going up to change before we deliver the cookies."

Their heads tilted together over the waffle cookie, the girls carefully sprinkled on the glitter.

"It's beautiful," Maddie sighed, eyes wide with wonder.

Penny carefully picked up the waffle to get a closer look, and all the glitter slid off.

"It's too slippy!" Maddie complained.

"It's because the frosting is dry," Penny said, looking around the kitchen. "We need something to make it stick."

French onion dip, grape jelly, a sprinkle of pickle juice, and a tiny spoonful of pumpkin pie whose hole they hid by nudging over the whipped cream splotch in the middle; nothing helped to make the cookie glitter stick.

"What's the stickiest thing on the whole earth?" Penny wondered aloud.

"Ooooh, I know," her little sister answered, "because I'm not allowed to have it because mom doesn't want to have to cut it out of my hair again." She scrambled up on the kitchen counter, opened a cabinet, and pulled something out that was hidden behind the flower vases.

"Bubble gum!" Penny exclaimed, helping her sister down and staring at the gum with glee. "Maddie, you're a genius!"

Her little sister grinned with pride.

"We're gonna have to chew it up really good," Penny said seriously, "to get it really, really sticky."

Maddie nodded gravely. "I promise I won't get any of it in my hair or ears or up my nose this time."

It was hard work, chewing gum for Santa. One piece after another, the girls chewed until each piece became a soft, gooey, slobbery, glob. Each glob had to then be carefully stretched and pressed onto the waffle. When every inch was covered with carefully chewed gum, the girls dumped the whole jar of sprinkles on top. "It'll help soak up the pickle juice," Penny assured Maddie as their mom came back into the kitchen.

"Wow!" their mom exclaimed, leaning over to examine the cookie waffle. She gave a tentative sniff. "It's... briny. But beautiful. Santa will love it!"

Hours later, cookies delivered to their neighbors, left-over pizza eaten in front of their favorite Christmas movie, and eyelids drooping with sleepiness, the girls carefully placed Santa's cookie waffle on the fireplace mantle. "It's a Santa Waffle Sparkle Spectacular," Penny announced with a happy sigh.

Reminded by their mom that Santa can't come in the middle of the night if kids are still awake, the girls slid off to their bedroom in their slippy-footed pjs.

Hours later, Penny was hanging over the top bunk, whispering her sister awake. "Maddie!" she whispered loudly. "Do you hear that?"

Her little sister opened her eyes and blinked. "Is it the middle of the night?" she mumbled in a sleepy voice.

"The middle *middle* of the night," Penny answered, swinging down from the top bunk and holding her hand out to her sister. "Let's go see if Santa ate the cookie waffle," she whispered.

Carefully opening their door so it wouldn't squeak, the girls padded down the hall in their matching red fuzzy footsie pajamas. The fire in the living room had gone out, but the Christmas tree lights cast a soft rainbow glow across the room. "It's very cozy," Penny observed approvingly as they tiptoed closer. Suddenly, she stopped, but Maddie didn't and bumped into her so hard they both tumbled into the living room.

They scrambled up, ducking behind the Christmas tree as they took in the scene before them. A round man with a fluffy white beard, dressed in a fuzzy red pajama-looking outfit of his own stood facing their stockings, which bulged and overflowed with glorious presents.

"It's Santa!" Maddie whisper-squealed. "AND HE'S GOING TO EAT OUR SANTA WAFFLE SPARKLE SPECATACULAR!" The second part wasn't so much a whisper as it was an excited shout.

Penny clapped her hand over her sister's mouth and pulled her further behind the tree as Santa turned around, their special cookie paused midway to his mouth. He stared at the Christmas tree, furrowed his fluffy white eyebrows, and then shrugged, turning back around. The sisters watched wide-eyed as Santa raised the cookie to his mouth and paused. Then, he sniffed. "Pickle juice?" they heard him ask in his deep jolly voice. "And..." he sniffed again. "Onion dip, grape jelly and..." he wrinkled his nose. "Pumpkin pie. But... it smells like just the teensiest bit." Then he opened wide and took a giant bite of their waffle cookie.

"He's chewing!" Penny whispered gleefully, as Santa chewed thoughtfully.

"He's still chewing!" Maddie added.

Santa chewed and chewed, his eyebrows first furrowing and then raising up in surprise. He kept chewing, and then stopped. Even with his fluffy beard and moustache, the girls could see he was moving his lips, squinching them side to side, then puckering, and then...

"He's blowing a bubble!" Maddie whispered, shaking Penny's arm with excitement.

Santa, they learned, is an expert bubble blower. The bubble started small, then grew and grew and grew until Santa made the "Oh, oh, oh!" sound that you make when you've blown an excellent bubble and want someone to see. The girls were just about to step out from the behind the tree, when... POP!

The giant bubble popped, sending glitter and bits of gum all over their stockings, all over the living room, and all over Santa.

Santa blinked.

The girls blinked.

Santa…. *glittered*. With two fingers he a pulled a chunk of gum from his beard. And then another from the furry white trim of his hat. And then he laughed, a jolly, deep laugh that echoed throughout the house as he disappeared up their chimney with a *whoosh*.

The next afternoon, after a morning of pulling treats out of stockings, exchanging presents, eating cinnamon buns, and taking naps among the torn wrapping paper under the tree, the sisters were gathered with their cousins in their grandmother's living room.

In the kitchen, their moms and aunts and uncles helped clear Christmas dinner from the table, and the cousins compared notes about their Christmas mornings.

"He comes to our houses after yours," their oldest cousin, Declan, said knowledgably to Maddie and Penny, "so you get your presents first."

"And then after Declan's, he comes to our place," their cousin Zoya said. "And then he goes to Meredith and Jacob's."

"Know what's weird?" Jacob asked, deciding he'd had enough of his tie, yanking it off and clipping it to a branch of the Christmas tree. "Our den was like …

covered in glitter this morning. My dad made us vacuum before we even got to the stockings."

Penny and Maddie exchanged a wide-eyed conspiratorial look.

"Hey, us too!" Declan exclaimed with wonder. "I mean, we didn't vacuum so it got everywhere, but there was a ton of pink and purple glitter."

"Oh, you mean like this?" Zoya said, shaking her head so a spray of glitter rained down. "I accidentally rolled in it," she smirked.

"How about you two," Jacob asked, looking at Maddie and Penny.

The sisters grinned at each other, keeping secret the note that had floated down the chimney as Santa left.

Thank you for the Santa Waffle Sparkle Spectacular.

(next time, leave out the pumpkin pie)

Xo
S.C.

5

THE SMALLEST REINDEER

S anta's elves are happy creatures born to work at the North Pole alongside one of the most famous beings in all of history and magic. They love making presents, toys, gadgets, and goodies for Santa to bring to all good girls and boys. And yes, elves are small, but they are just the right size for swiveling small screwdrivers, tinkering with tiny toys, and preparing petite presents. In fact, they don't want to be taller any more than we humans want to be smaller because of how much they love their jobs.

But there was one creature who was small but felt he shouldn't be. This wasn't because he didn't like being little, but because he was a reindeer. Now, all the North Pole reindeer had the prestigious honor of being a part of Santa's team of helpers to make Christmas perfect each year. Some of the most famous reindeer were those who pulled the sleigh through the snowy winter sky on Christmas Eve. But others had jobs that were just as important, like helping carry sleighs full of equipment for building toys or pulling Mrs. Claus's sleigh full of treats around the North Pole. These jobs required the North Pole's magical reindeer to be regular-sized and especially strong, but Kleiner, the little reindeer, was neither.

You see, on the fateful day Kleiner was born, the weather was unusually cold and blustery. Each year on the first day of winter, the North Pole throws a big party to celebrate the start of the season. Every elf, reindeer, snowman, yeti, and even Mr. and Mrs. Claus get dressed in their best winter hats and ugliest Christmas sweaters to party like it's Christmas morning. They all cheer as Old Man Winter, the living spirit of the season, kicks off the party by blowing his icy breath across the sky and land, blanketing the ground with snow and turning ponds to ice. Once the winter party has begun, Old Man Winter always makes a quick exit to prepare for the rest of the season.

The party festivities include snow angel-making, snowball fights, ice skating, dancing, caroling, hot chocolate-drinking, cookie-eating, and storytelling, all beneath the glow of endless strands of Christmas lights. The party usually lasts all day and late into the night. But this year, when the hour grew late, rather than end the party, Donner and Blitzen, well-known for their partying, sought out Old Man Winter again. They found him working hard to keep the cold winter breezes flowing all the way until springtime.

The pair asked the old man if he would come back and blow the icy winter magic across the sky again, but he said no. "I'm far too busy; we have a whole season ahead of us," he told them.

The two rambunctious partiers glanced at each other and knew precisely what to say.

"Santa didn't want to say anything, but we could tell he was really bummed the party was ending. We thought it would be a great surprise for him if we came to ask you to make an afterparty," said Blitzen, thinking on his feet.

Old Man Winter stroked his flowing beard as he pondered the idea. Suddenly he looked up at the waiting reindeer and nodded. "Okay. For Santa, I will do it! And I'll make it the most wintry afterparty you've ever seen," boomed Old Man Winter.

The reindeer nodded excitedly and flew off to rejoin the waning party. The Clauses were about to leave when Old Man Winter reappeared in the sky above. He grinned as he blew the strongest winter breeze he'd blown in years across the North Pole. The partygoers cheered again, and the Christmas lights burned brighter as the party began anew.

"What's all this?" asked Santa with a chuckle. As he looked up into the wonderful winter sky, he clutched his hat so the powerful wind wouldn't blow it right off his head. And though he was pleased and the party continued, the same icy wind blew well into the next day, when a special reindeer was born.

Now, of course, Santa's reindeer are unique and powered by the holiday magic that flows through all things at the North Pole. But each type of magical being in the North Pole has its own specific kind of magic that ensures it becomes the elf, reindeer, or snowman it's supposed to be. For example, the elves' holiday magic makes them small, pointy-eared, and everything else that comes with being an elf. And even better, their magic looks like brightly colored sprinkles and smells like a warm sugar cookie!

Well, the chilly winds from the winter afterparty were still blowing so hard the following day that a bit of this magic meant for the elves blew over to where the reindeer lived and mixed with reindeer magic.

The only reindeer born this day was very tiny, so his parents named him Kleiner, which means *small*. Since all reindeer start off pretty small, no one noticed anything unusual at first. But reindeer in the North Pole grow very quickly, yet as time passed and Christmases passed, Kleiner remained very small. Being small didn't bother Kleiner much because he loved Christmas and was more than happy to be one of Santa's reindeer living at the North Pole. He quickly made friends with the other reindeer and, after meeting Rudolph, looked up to him as his personal hero. Despite his size, his Christmas joy was enormous and after witnessing his first Christmas, Kleiner began training to become part of the following year's celebration.

He would begin each day by observing some of the other reindeer as they performed their duties. Kleiner would watch them closely and take notes on everything they did so he could use his notes later during his training. The reindeer all got to know him and liked when he would watch them, as he often cheered them on and flattered them with questions about their jobs. His Christmas spirit was truly inspirational, and he was so small, he never got in the way of their work.

It was only when Kleiner tried helping the other reindeer that he ran into trouble. He always meant well and knew how to do the jobs, but he just couldn't match the strength of the bigger reindeer. When one went on break, Kleiner would try to fill in and even rigged the giant harness to fit around his body. Yet when it came time to pull the sleigh, Kleiner couldn't manage. When the reindeer who'd taken a break returned, he could see the disappointment on Kleiner's face.

"It's okay, Kleiner," consoled the reindeer, "maybe one day you'll grow into it."

"Yeah, maybe," said Kleiner with a smile. It quickly faded though, as he wriggled out of the regular reindeer-sized harness. Things went on this way for months as Kleiner studied other reindeer and trained hard, flying against the strongest winds and lifting weights to try and become strong enough to help pull a sleigh.

Then it came time for the next holiday season. Tryouts for all the roles in making Christmas would be held before everyone got down to the actual work. Every type of creature at the North Pole had to perform a certain task, and to ensure Christmas went smoothly, Santa needed everyone to be in the jobs they were best suited for. Alas, tryouts didn't go very well for Kleiner. Despite his hard work, he still couldn't pull a sleigh or lift a load like the other reindeer. At the end of the day, Kleiner's name wasn't on any of the boards assigning him to a task. He wasn't strong enough to do a reindeer's job and didn't have the crafty hands of an elf.

"Don't worry, kid," said the head reindeer, "we'll get creative and find something for you to do." But no one ever did, and as Christmas Eve neared, Kleiner grew sad. He didn't even show up to cheer on the other reindeer in the final weeks before Christmas as they practiced for the big night. Instead, he stayed in bed and watched Christmas movies all day, but even they reminded him that he couldn't help with the most wonderful time of the year.

Everyone at the North Pole gathered together for a reading of *The Night Before Christmas* on Christmas Eve. Not even being sad could keep Kleiner from one of the most important gatherings of the season. He took a seat among the other reindeer, but when the story began, he crawled between them to a spot where he could see better. There at the front of the crowd, he had a perfect view of Mrs. Claus and the reindeer from the story who were gathered together for the reading by Santa. As Santa read the story of visiting houses and delivering presents, Kleiner had an idea.

Later that night, the elves helped the reindeer strap in and put the final touches on the sleigh as Santa sat down and took the reins. As the clock struck midnight and Santa took off with Rudolph in the lead, Kleiner was nowhere to be found. The sleigh flew through the night and made its way across the sky to the first house on the list. Santa landed on the rooftop and stepped out of the sleigh to grab the presents for the children in the house below. He checked his list, loaded into his sack the toys, balls, dolls, and games the "nice" children had asked for and slung it over his shoulder before starting down the chimney.

As he made his way down the chimney, he noticed how clean it was. *Ah, one of the nice ones*, he thought happily as he popped out the bottom. He quickly glanced down at his bright red suit, and there wasn't a stain on it.

"Looks good, right?" said Kleiner enthusiastically. Santa was used to the occasional boy or girl waking up in the middle of the night, but the voice still made him jump. He turned, and there flying in front of him, was a little reindeer wearing a chimney brush around his midsection.

"Ho, ho, ho, there. Hmm, yes, it does indeed!" Santa boomed. Kleiner beamed. "And who might you be, little one?"

"Kleiner, sir, reporting for duty as your official chimney climber," said Kleiner proudly.

"You mean you climbed down the chimney and cleaned it just now?" asked Santa.

Kleiner nodded. "To protect your suit, Santa," chirped Kleiner.

Santa looked again at his spotless red suit. "Job well done, my young friend, and creative thinking too. Since it's your official job now, though, do you mind if I call you "Climber"?"

Kleiner spun around in a circle, and tears began to well in his eyes. "I'd like that very much, Santa, sir."

"Well then, welcome to the team, Climber! Now let's get back to work. We've got a lot of houses to visit." With that, Santa turned and began pulling gifts from his sack on the floor and placing them under the tree. Before he could reach down for another, Climber presented him with a pair of new skates from the sack.

"Here you go," said Climber, holding them up at eye level.

Santa smiled. "Ah, those go there," said Santa, pointing below a red stocking that hung from the fireplace. As Climber gently set the skates down, Santa realized he now had a partner for when he delivered gifts. From that day forward, Climber went with Santa down every chimney, helping him deliver presents and ensuring his red suit always stayed clean.

6

A-CAROLING WE SHALL GO

Dusk had fallen, and nine-year-old Clara quietly switched on the Christmas candle in her grandmother's bedroom window, peering out into the darkness of the front yard and the neighborhood beyond.

Clara smiled as in house after house, candles flickered on in the windows and colorful strings of holiday lights lit up bushes, mailboxes, front doors, and window frames. Clara's favorite decorations, though, were the candles. The solitary flickering flames – battery operated of course – in each window made her feel somehow equally full of coziness and longing.

"I love watching the candles go on," Clara's grandmother said from where she lay in bed.

"Oh no, did I wake you?" Clara whispered, turning to smile at her grandmother. "I tried to tiptoe…"

"I was done napping ages ago," her grandmother said, sitting up and swinging her legs over the side of the bed. "Your father seems to think napping will cure what ails me and sends me to my room just like I used to do to him when he was an overtired little boy," she smirked.

Clara's grandmother hadn't always lived with them. She'd lived in a little apartment in a retirement community a few hours away, close to Clara's Aunt Veronica. Clara and her family would visit Grandma on holidays, and Grandma would come to stay with them for a week or so in the summer. But in the spring, Grandma had what Clara's father gravely referred to as *a fall* at her apartment, and it was decided she should come and live with them.

Even though Clara knew her grandmother, she still felt shy around her at first. Having someone visit you is a lot different than having that person move in. Clara helped set up the guest room with her grandmother's things, and on the day her grandmother came home from the hospital, Clara had left a bouquet of flowers from the front yard on the nightstand.

She'd stayed in her bedroom, peeking out as her parents helped Grandma down the hall. Grandma had a walker now, and it seemed like it was hard for her to take steps. She looked... different. Clara's parents hovered on either side of her until her grandmother suddenly stopped.

"Are you okay, Mom?" her parents asked in unison, their arms outstretched as if ready to catch her. Clara worried her grandmother was going to fall.

"My dears, if you don't stop buzzing around me like bees, I'm afraid you're going to get stung!"

Clara giggled, then covered her mouth and ducked into her room. That was her grandmother all right. Clara peeked out again just as her grandmother turned to look at her and wink before saying to Clara's parents, "I will see my room now, thank you."

It wasn't long before Clara couldn't remember a time when her grandmother hadn't lived with them. Spring had turned to summer, and summer to fall, and now Christmas was just a few days away.

Clara took her grandmother's outstretched hand and helped her to the chair by the window. "Do you want me to turn on a light?" she asked, as her grandmother settled into the chair.

"Oh no, dear," replied her grandmother, "I think I'll leave them off, just for a while longer. That way we can see all the lights glowing in the darkness. It looks like a constellation of colorful stars don't you think?"

Clara sat on the edge of the chair and nodded. "I think it might snow tonight," she said. "Maybe it will be a big storm and we'll have three snow days in a row and then it will be Christmas!"

"Maybe," her grandmother said, patting Clara's hand, falling into a long silence. Finally, she said, "I can almost hear the singing."

"The singing?" Clara asked, confused. She strained her ears but heard nothing outside apart from the occasional bark of a dog or passing car.

"When I was a little girl, on nights like this when you could smell snow in the air and just *feel* that Christmas was coming, we would go caroling."

"Christmas caroling?" Clara asked. "Like the winter choral concert at school?"

Clara had been so proud to see her grandmother sitting with her parents in the audience. She had been too shy to try out for a solo, but she had sung every note for her grandmother, as if it was just the two of them there.

"Oh, many of the same songs. But we would go outside together and sing for our neighbors."

"I've seen that in movies," Clara said.

"I'm sure you have. It was a wonderful way to spread the Christmas spirit. Sometimes neighbors would bring out hot chocolate or treats, and sometimes they would join us in caroling."

"Why don't people do it anymore?" Clara wondered aloud.

"The world has changed," her grandmother explained. "I'm sure some people still go caroling, but people seem more inclined to just... well, keep their joy to themselves."

"That's sad," Clara noted, looking out the window and thinking of all her neighbors, together in their neighborhood, but each all on their own.

"It is sad," her grandmother agreed. "Because it is amazing what joy can do when it spreads."

"So why doesn't anyone do that, Grandma? You know, spread the joy?"

"Oh, all sorts of reasons," her grandmother answered. "Fear, mostly, I think. It's scary to open that door to people."

"The door to your house?" Clara asked, again confused.

"Well, yes, the door to your house, but also the door to your joy, to your heart," her grandmother observed. "When we would gather to sing carols - *O holy night* was my favorite - we were opening the door to our hearts and asking our neighbors to share in our joy. And in turn, they opened the doors to their homes and did the same."

"What's so scary about opening a door?" Clara asked, but really, she already knew the answer. At school, she was friendly with almost everybody. She had kids she sat with at lunch and could usually find someone to pair up with for group projects, but it made her very nervous to even think about doing something like inviting someone over after school. After all, *what if they said no?* she thought.

Her grandmother squeezed her hand lovingly. "Sometimes, when we're scared, the best thing we can do is open that door."

The two stared out the window in happy silence as a flurry of snow swirled in the wind, glowing in the moonlight.

"What's happened to Grandma?" Clara asked with alarm the next afternoon when she got home from school. "Is she okay?"

Much to her disappointment, last night's snow had disappeared by morning, and off to school she had gone. But when she got home, her parents were there to greet her, which is how she knew right off that something was wrong.

"Grandma will be fine," Clara's mom assured her. "She's just feeling a little worn out. Dad's gotten her settled for a nap, and we're waiting for a call back from her doctor."

"She doesn't need a nap," Clara insisted, heading down the hall toward her grandmother's room. "I bet she's wide awake in there."

Clara pushed open the door to the darkened room and stopped. Her dad had moved the chair that had been next to the window so he could sit beside his mother's bed and hold her hand as she slept. He looked up at Clara. "Grandma's just a little tired," he whispered.

Out the window, dusk was falling, and Clara watched as one by one, the candles flickered on in her neighbors' windows.

"Dad, I'm going outside for a little bit," she whispered as she got an idea, and she softly closed the bedroom door.

Clara gulped. Her stomach was full of butterflies, and even though she was bundled up in a coat, hat, mittens, and scarf, she shivered.

"This was a bad idea," she whispered to herself, as she stared up the steps leading to her neighbor's front door. The colorful lights strung all over the house and bushes cast a warm, colorful glow.

Clara cleared her throat. *O holy night...* she sang. Her voice sounded so small; it wavered and cracked. She started again.

O holy night, the stars are brightly shining.

She stopped singing and watched the front door, half hoping and half scared it would open.

It is the eve... of our dear savior's birth.

Soft snow began to fall. She stopped singing again, watching the door, but it didn't open.

"I tried, Grandma," she whispered, turning to walk back to her house.

"Hey!" called a voice behind her.

Clara turned and saw a kid her own age standing in the open doorway, holding a piece of pizza.

"Was that you singing?" he asked, shoving half the pizza in his mouth.

"Um…" Clara said shyly, "Yes?"

"Why are you singing on our doorstep?" he asked with his mouth full.

"I'm… caroling," she said, feeling a little foolish.

"Like in the movies?" he asked with surprise, polishing off his slice of pizza. "Hey, you're Clara, right? You sang at the winter show. I'm Jacob."

"I know," Clara nodded, "we've been neighbors for like… ever."

Jacob shrugged. "Well, I like your voice."

"Thanks," Clara smiled faintly, not sure what to say next.

"So, you're just like… singing at people's houses? Doesn't caroling usually involve more than one person?"

"Yes," Clara answered more crossly than she'd meant to. "You wanna come?"

Jacob wiped pizza grease off his hand onto his sweat-pants and considered her offer. "Sure," he said finally, calling into the house, "Mom, I'm going caroling! Back soon!"

Clara was stunned. She hadn't considered that he would actually say *yes*. A few minutes later, Jacob joined her on the front walk, wearing his coat and hat.

"Where to next?" he asked, sounding excited.

"Um…" Clara thought, "I guess the Parkers?"

"Cool," Jacob nodded as they walked toward the Parkers' house. "So what should we sing? I don't know that one you were singing before. I know 'Jingle Bells,' though."

"'Jingle Bells' works," she agreed, smiling as Jacob leaped into the air to try and catch a snowflake on his tongue.

Singing with Jacob was different from singing with the choral group. For one thing, his notes were all over the place, and he was LOUD. But as they stood together singing on the Parker's front porch, with its giant inflatable Santa Claus that Jacob kept high-fiving as he sang, it was obvious that he was really enjoying himself. When the front door swung open, Jacob let out a whoop so loud Clara forgot the words and burst out laughing.

"What's all this?" Mrs. Parker asked as she stood in the doorway smiling. "Clara, everything okay at your house?"

"Yes, Mrs. Parker," Clara answered, "my grandmother's just a little worn out, so I'm... I'm caroling to cheer her up."

"You didn't tell me that," Jacob said, his brow wrinkling with concern. "Is she okay?"

Clara nodded. "She'll be okay."

"Well can I join you kids?" Mrs. Parker asked, "I haven't gone caroling since I was a little girl!"

"Sure!" exclaimed Clara happily. "That would be great!"

"And let me get Mr. Parker, even though he'll bring us down a whole octave. Barry!" she called into the house. "We're going caroling!"

"Way ahead of you," Mr. Parker boomed, appearing at the door. He handed Mrs. Parker her coat and put on his own. "A-caroling we shall go," he said enthusiastically.

This time, they sang as they walked through the falling snow, and as they climbed the front steps of the

Gilbert's house singing, "We wish you a merry Christmas," the Gilberts were already standing in their open doorway grinning. In fact, house after house welcomed Clara and her growing chorus, cheering them on and then joining them until there was only one house left to visit.

"This is your place, isn't it?" Jacob asked as they gathered at the foot of Clara's front walk.

She nodded.

"What shall we sing?" asked Mrs. Gilbert.

"We should sing that one you were singing at my house," Jacob suggested. "I don't know it, but I liked the way you sang it."

"It's my grandmother's favorite," Clara said softly, blushing.

"Then it's perfect," Jacob said and everyone smiled.

Clara swallowed and took a deep breath. *O holy night,* she sang, and her voice didn't sound small anymore because it wasn't just her voice doing the singing, *the stars are brightly shining.*

They were all singing.

It is the night of our dear Savior's birth.

Clara's front door opened and her mom and dad appeared, their expressions filled with surprise and joy. But as they sang on, Clara's eyes were on her grandmother's window, where a single candle flickered. *Fall on your knees,* she sang, vaguely aware that the other voices around her had quieted. *O hear the angel voices!*

In the window, a silhouette appeared, the candle lighting up her face. Clara's grandmother smiled down at them, her lips moving as she sang along.

…O night, when Christ was born.

O night, O holy night, O night divine!

Later, after her neighbors had all come inside for hot cocoa and cookies, and after she and Jacob had made plans to build a humungous snowman the following day, Clara slipped into her grandmother's room.

"Hello, darling," her grandmother said from where she lay in bed. "What a wonderful surprise that was."

Clara curled up beside her grandmother, her eyelids growing heavy as her grandmother stroked her hair. "I opened the door, Grandma," she said sleepily.

"And you shared the joy," her grandmother nodded proudly.

7

AN ELF FOR CHRISTMAS

One cold, stormy night, the glow of light coming from Santa's workshop could be seen through the thick snow. If you come a little closer, you'll even hear hammers pounding, machines whirring, and little elf feet scurrying.

"I know you've all put in a lot of long hours this week, but Christmas is only two days away, and we still have a lot to do!" Manager Elf was trying to motivate his crew, as he rubbed his tired eyes. The elves had been working overtime the whole week because a few days ago there had been a slight delay in production. During the elf Christmas party, everyone drank some hot cocoa that had gone bad, and they were all out sick for three days!

Now it was almost midnight, and production was slower than ever. The toy car assembling elves were putting steering wheels where the tires were supposed to go. The doll-assembling elves were having a hard time putting the arms and legs in the right places. One elf, in particular, was so tired that he kept falling asleep at the assembly line. He was a gift-wrapping elf called Eddy. Eddy's job was to take the toys that came off the assembly line and put them on the conveyer belt to be gift-wrapped.

Eddy's eyes stayed closed a little longer each time he blinked, until he didn't open them anymore and silently snored while standing. His body started going limp, and he lay down on the gift-wrapping conveyer belt. The relaxing movement of the belt put him into an even deeper sleep. He was unaware that the gift-wrapping machine was carefully putting him into a red box with a green bow. The box, with him inside, softly landed on top of the pile in the giant red sack.

Manager elf was walking through the assembly lines and saw that the wooden horses looked more like wooden hippos, and the toy dogs meowed instead of barked. "Stop what you're doing!" he yelled over the pounding of hammers and whirring of machines. "I've decided to call it a night before any more toys are messed up." The elves all breathed a sigh of relief and put their tools down. They slowly walked out, and the lights went out in Santa's workshop. Eddy the elf was still fast asleep under his blanket of tissue paper inside the gift box.

The next morning, the elves were feeling refreshed and knew that the end was in sight.

Christmas was tomorrow, and ever since they'd started making toys, they'd been looking forward to Christmas morning! Christmas morning is always a special time for the elves. They don't celebrate with gifts or toys. Instead, they all come together and sing songs. After singing, they all gather in Santa and Mrs. Claus' kitchen and have the most wonderful feast you can imagine. When all their little elf bellies are full, they play reindeer games. There wasn't an elf in the North Pole who wasn't looking forward to Christmas morning.

That whole day the elves worked hard to finish the final gifts and make sure they made it to the pile in Santa's big red sack. No one seemed to notice that Eddy was not where he was supposed to be.

That night, as Santa was putting on his red suit and combing his beard, the big red sack with all the gifts was being closed by a tall crane-like machine, and then put on Santa's sleigh. The movement startled Eddy, and he finally woke up. At first, he didn't know where he was, but as Santa lined up his reindeer and started calling out their names, he figured it out. "Oh no, oh no, oh no! Santa! Saaaantaaaa!" Eddy yelled, but the reindeer had already started to take off to deliver gifts to the children of the world.

Santa's first stop was in Europe and Asia. Next, he went down under to deliver gifts to Australian children and to other small islands. Every time Santa stopped to deliver a gift, Eddy would rattle his box and call out to Santa, but Santa didn't seem to notice. His next stops were Africa and the Middle East. When Eddy started to sweat, he knew they must be far south. Their last stops were North and South America, and finally, Santa grabbed the red box with the green bow. It was dark, and all Eddy could hear were sleigh bells. Santa dropped down the chimney and put Eddy under a beautiful Christmas tree. He took one of the cookies and a sip of the milk that had been left for him and set off to finish his last few deliveries.

As Santa made his way up the chimney, he knocked over a piece of wood that startled Layla, a small brown shaggy dog who was sleeping near the fireplace. She came to investigate. Under the tree, the red box with a green bow started moving. Curious, Layla moved closer to investigate. The box moved again, and this time the lid popped off, making Layla jump and yelp. Eddy climbed out and looked around in wonder, fascinated by his surroundings. He had never been in a human house before. He saw Layla and immediately recognized her. She had been the family's gift seven years ago! Eddy had wrapped her up himself, after being slobbered on by the adorable little puppy.

Eddy walked over to Layla and patted her on the head. She seemed to remember Eddy too because she wagged her tail and gave him a big old slobbery lick. Layla was very happy to see Eddy. She'd been a little lonely lately and had no one to play with.

Eddy started looking around to see if he could find any clues as to where he might be. He needed to find his way back to the North Pole. He didn't want to miss Christmas. The snow outside suggested he was somewhere north. He saw a letter on the floor below the mail slot in the front door and quickly ran over.

1819 Hardy Road
Yorkton, Saskatchewan
Canada

"Okay, Canada… I can work with Canada. At least it's not South Africa or Australia; otherwise, I would never make it on time." He started pacing the living room, thinking of a way to get home. Layla, her tongue hanging out and tail wagging, started pacing with him. Eddy saw a map of the world on the wall and climbed onto Layla's back to get a closer look. "So, I need to get more north, then go east all the way to Greenland, then from there make my way up to the North Pole," he whispered to himself.

He jumped off Layla's back and started pacing again. He had no idea how he was going do it. He thought of taking a toy car, but it would take forever to get there. Then he thought of taking a real car, but he quickly put that scary thought out of his head. Just then, Layla started pacing with him again, and he got a brilliant idea. "You can help me get home, Layla!" he exclaimed happily.

Layla started wagging her tail excitedly, almost hitting poor Eddy. Eddy noticed that she had a little Christmas sweater hanging by the front door, so he hopped onto the table to try and retrieve it. He struggled to get it on her, but eventually she sat still long enough for him to put it on. He jumped on Layla's back and whispered in her ear to go and off they went, through the doggy door, up the street, and out of town!

Eddy had about six hours left before the first Christmas songs, and he had no intention of missing even a single note. Layla kept a steady pace for a long time but after a while began to grow tired. Eddy saw a bus stop ahead and steered her towards it. He read the sign on the front of the bus that said where it was going.

Nunavut

He was pretty sure Nunavut was close to Greenland, so he and Layla scrambled into the luggage compartment without being seen just as it was being closed by the driver. It was quite a long drive, and Eddy's stomach started to rumble. He realized he hadn't eaten anything all day. Layla started sniffing around the bags and found a box of Christmas cookies. They both had a few cookies and dozed off. Eddy woke up as the bus came to a stop. As soon as the luggage compartment opened, Eddy and Layla jumped out. In front of the bus station was a huge map and Eddy started planning out the rest of their journey. "… mmm hmmm, west… okay, five miles… north… two hours… airplane… mmm… 17 miles. " Eddy was mumbling to himself as he made the calculations in his head.

"Okay, here's the plan, Layla. We're going to go to the airport, which is five miles west of here. There are always pilots flying at this time of day so they can be with their families on Christmas. We're going to get on an airplane and fly two hours north to Greenland.

From Greenland, it's about 17 miles to the North Pole. If my calculations are correct, we'll be there by sunrise.

Eddy held on tight as Layla sped off. They found the airport, just like Eddy had said, and even found an airplane that said 'Greenland Transport Inc.' They jumped into the cockpit as the pilot untied the airplane, and they hid under the passenger seat. The pilot started the engine, and they were off. Two hours later, they landed in Greenland and quickly jumped out when the pilot opened the door. They ran and ran until they reached the shores of the ocean. Eddy knew he was close, but he had no idea how to cross the icy ocean.

The sun was starting to peak over the water's edge, and Eddy felt defeated. Just as he was losing all hope, a giant polar bear came strolling toward them. She was a strange-looking polar bear; she wasn't pure white like most of the others, and she had brown spots on her ears and a brown heart-shaped spot on her body.

At first, Eddy was scared because she was so large, but then he saw the gentleness in her eyes, and somehow, he knew she had come to help. She bent her front legs, almost as if she was bowing, and motioned for them both to jump up on her back. Eddy and Layla climbed on, a little nervous, but she slowly moved into the ice water, leaving only her back and her new friends above the water line and then she started to swim.

It took them about an hour to reach the North Pole. When they finally reached land, they were greeted with cheers and applause. It turned out that Santa had sent Lucy the polar bear to find Eddy and bring him home!

Everyone, including Layla and Lucy, went to the town square to sing songs. Then they went to the Claus' house for their wonderful Christmas feast. As they all sat around the table, Santa said: "Layla, thank you for bringing our Eddy back safely where he belonged. There is a special gift waiting for you when you return home."

Layla wagged her tail and resumed her feast of dog biscuits, peanut butter, and pumpkin pie. After the feast, everyone went to watch the reindeer games. After the reindeer games, Santa came up to Eddy and Layla. "My dear Eddy, it's time for Layla to go home now." A single tear ran down Eddy's cheek, but Layla quickly licked it away. He kissed her on the head and Santa picked her up and walked away.

Since Santa didn't have millions of presents to deliver anymore, he only needed one reindeer, and climbed onto his sleigh with his red bag that seemed to be empty, and Layla. They soon arrived at Layla's house and Santa put the sleeping dog in her bed beside the fireplace. He also put a gift under the tree.

When Layla opened her eyes, there was a red box with a green bow. Inside was a white puppy with brown spots on her ears and a brown heart-shaped spot on her body. Her tag read 'Lucy'. Layla yelped and bounced around with joy at the sight of her new playmate.

8

THE BEST GIFT

Christmas was here! Siblings Tom, Maya, Adam, and Rachel had all made their Christmas wish lists and couldn't wait to open their gifts. The colorful wrapping, the twinkly lights, the delicious treats – everything about the holiday was so exciting! Even the smells everywhere were Christmasy.

Tom, the eldest, loved sports so much that his bed was shaped like a football. Mom liked to call him a sports nut, but Dad thought he might one day inspire other kids to follow their passion. Naturally, Tom's list was filled with sports-related stuff, like a soccer ball and a new baseball mitt.

Maya loved fashion and beautiful clothes and dreamed of becoming a famous fashion designer. She could already knit and crochet, but she wanted to learn how to create designs and work with all kinds of fabrics. Mom liked the idea but hoped she would only use sustainable materials. Maya's wish list included dolls she could dress up and fancy new clothes for herself.

As for Adam, he loved nature, science and astronomy. Ever since he'd been a toddler, his favorite thing to do was to stand on his tiptoes and stare at the moon through Dad's telescope. He was so filled with curiosity that he wanted to learn everything he could about everything he saw. Mom thought Adam might discover something one day that would benefit the whole world. Adam liked thinking about that idea and added a telescope and microscope to his Christmas wish list.

Rachel was the youngest of the siblings. She hadn't learned to write very well yet, but she loved to draw pictures and to make things, though she was sometimes unsure what she was making until after she had finished it. Mom and Dad were sure she would one day be a celebrated artist like Rembrandt or Frida Kahlo. She would use color to make the world more beautiful. Rachel's list included crayons and colored pencils, as well as a giant sketchbook where she could sketch her ideas.

"Guys, Daddy and I need your help," Mom said to the children. "We need to think of something extra special for Granny and Pop Pop. We thought maybe we could have a gift-giving contest, and that each of you could come up with an idea about what to give them. What do you think?" she asked the children, as they beamed with joy at the thought.

"I have an idea!" exclaimed Tom instantly.

"Me too!" piped up Maya, determined to keep pace with her older brother.

"So do I!" said Adam, not wanting to feel left out.

"I don't, but I will," squeaked little Rachel.

"That's wonderful," smiled Mom, clasping her hands together. "Dad and I will help you with your ideas."

They would be visiting Granny and Pop-pop on Christmas in just a week, so they started working on their gift ideas right away.

Tom knew his grandparents loved photos of their grandchildren. Pop-pop always asked for pictures of him playing soccer and baseball. He even had a 'Sports Wall,' where he hung all the photos of Tom playing the many sports he was involved in. Both grandparents even came to many of his sporting events to cheer him on. So for his gift to them, Tom found the most comfortable camp chairs he could find online and had his picture printed on the backs. This way, his grandparents could attend his events in comfort and style. He was quite proud of his idea.

Maya searched for the softest sustainable wool in Granny and Pop-pop's favorite colors. She knitted them matching hats and scarves to keep them warm and stylish all winter. "These are stunning," Mom complimented as she admired Maya's handiwork. The colors were vibrant, and the patterns were beautiful.

"I designed them myself," Maya said proudly, believing her gift for her grandparents to be the most thoughtful.

Adam used his love of nature to create his gift, and put together a leaf collection. Collecting and identifying leaves and feathers was one of his favorite activities that he did with his grandparents. Thanks to them, he could name a whole bunch of plants and figure out which birds the feathers had come from. His grand-mother had even taught him how to press and preserve them and he now had a large collection. So for his gift, Adam made a scrapbook of pressed plants, and labeled each specimen. He thought it looked very professional, and knew his grandparents would be impressed.

Little Rachel still hadn't come up with her gift idea. But she noticed that Tom, Maya, and Adam had all used their unique skills to create their gifts, so she decided to draw her grandparents a picture. It was a lovely drawing of her grandparents sitting on the beach, watching the sea. The next day, however, Rachel watched as Maya wrapped her scarves and hats in soft, shiny paper, and Rachel felt like her picture wasn't enough of a gift. She dug through her treasure boxes in her bedroom to find something else and pulled out some old photos of her and her family, shells she'd picked up on the beach, and feathers she'd found during walks in the forest. She carefully positioned the photos, feathers and shells around her drawing and her mom helped her glue them to make a frame.

"I hope they like it," Rachel whispered nervously as she wrapped her gift.

On Christmas day, the whole family headed to Granny and Pop-pop's house with their special gifts. Granny and Pop-pop greeted them at the door with hugs and kisses and delicious warm cookies, and the tree in the living room sparkled with colorful lights and shiny ornaments of all shapes and sizes. Their home smelled of pine and chocolate and pumpkin pie – all the wonderful smells of Christmas.

"So, we have a bit of a contest going," Mom announced to Granny and Pop-pop.

"Yes," interjected Dad, "who gives the best gift?" he laughed.

"Oh my!" said Granny. "Well, let's get started then and see who wins," she winked.

Tom went first and presented his camp chairs.

"Oh Tom, these will be perfect for watching you play!" Granny and Pop-pop agreed happily, admiring Tom's photo on the backs.

"And everyone will know who we're rooting for," laughed Pop-pop. "Such handsome pictures," he said, "Thank you, Tom, what a wonderful idea!"

Maya was next to present her gift.

"Oh, look at this wrapping paper!" Granny gasped. "Why it's almost too pretty to unwrap!"

she exclaimed as Maya blushed. But once they'd unwrapped the scarves and hats, Granny and Pop-pop modeled Maya's creations. "These are magnificent," Granny declared enthusiastically.

"Maya, your granny and pop-pop will be the warmest and most fashionable people around," said Pop-pop lovingly as he admired himself in the hall mirror.

Then it was time for Adam to present his plant book. Granny and Pop-pop eagerly turned the pages, awed by Adam's meticulous and thorough work. "Fantastic specimens, Adam, my boy," Pop-pop praised.

"What a brilliant idea," Granny marveled. "Thank you so much, sweetheart!" She kissed him as she had the others before him.

Finally, young Rachel presented her drawing. "Oh, dear," Granny croaked, her eyes became teary.

"Wow," Pop-pop whispered.

"Are you okay?" Rachel squeaked, worried that her gift had upset them.

"Oh, honey, I'm wonderful," Granny assured her with a broad smile.

"Those are happy tears, little one," Pop-pop explained as he put his arm around Rachel, "because your gift is so beautiful and thoughtful."

"So… do you have a favorite gift?" Adam asked Granny and Pop-pop as all four children anxiously waited for their decision. Mom and Dad smiled knowingly.

"We do," Granny answered with a nod.

"It's a four-way tie," Pop-pop announced.

"The best gift ever came in four parts," Granny explained.

"And each part was given to us by our greatest gifts ever," Pop-pop continued, "you four wonderful children." Granny and Pop-pop pulled all the children to them for a group hug as Mom and Dad looked on, grinning.

On the way home, the family talked about their Christmas with their grandparents. "Did you have fun?" Mom asked.

"We had a great time, Mom," Tom said sincerely.

"It was the best day ever," declared Adam with certainty.

"Me too," yawned Rachel, too sleepy to pay much attention.

"My favorite part was giving Granny and Pop-pop our gifts," said Maya, "and then hearing that we were their best gift ever," she beamed.

They all agreed, before the children fell asleep in the car, exhausted after such a long, festive, happy Christmas. When they arrived home, Mom and Dad shepherded them to their rooms, Dad carrying little Rachel, who was sound asleep, and put them to bed, where they would dream of Christmases to come.

9

DEAR SANTA, PLEASE PICK UP JINGLE!

It was Christmas Eve, and siblings Molly and Max were excitedly preparing for Santa's visit.

Molly laid out a tray of sugar cookies shining with red and green frosting. Beside it, her little brother Max placed a tall glass of icy cold milk—some of which might have been spilled on the long walk from the kitchen.

"Ready!" the children shouted merrily. They couldn't believe that Santa would be there so soon—and that he would snack on their special treats!

"Now wait a minute," said Dad with a frown as he and Mom came in and looked at the cookies and milk. "What about the reindeer? Haven't you left anything for them?"

"The reindeer?" asked Max.

"Reindeer can't have *cookies,* Dad," Molly said as she scrunched up her face.

"Maybe not cookies," agreed Mom, "But Santa's reindeer spend all night pulling his sleigh. They deserve a little snack, too, don't they?"

Agreeing, Max and Molly ran to the kitchen pantry to see what kinds of reindeer snacks they could find. Max pulled out a clipped-up crinkly bag. "Potato chips?" he suggested.

Molly shook her head. "I don't think so."

"Cheesy crackers?"

Molly shook her head again.

"Hmmm," mused Max, moving to the fridge. "Oh!" he exclaimed, "How about a Jell-O cup?"

Molly laughed. "No way."

"You know, I think reindeer eat a lot of the same things that horses do," Dad added helpfully as he watched them from the kitchen doorway.

But all the apples had been used up for apple pie. And all of the cranberries and raisins had been baked into Mom's cranberry-raisin stuffing.

"How about this?" asked Max, digging deep into the fridge's nearly-empty vegetable bin. He produced a tiny, withered old carrot. "It's the last one," said Max with a shrug.

Molly threw up her hands. "It'll have to do, I guess."

"Yes, it will," said Mom, who had joined Dad in the doorway, "Because it's time for bed."

Molly and Max rushed to deposit the tiny old carrot next to the tray with Santa's cookies and milk. They kissed their parents good night and paraded up the stairs to bed.

Before the sun was even up, Max was out of bed and poking at Molly. "Pssst," he whispered to his sister, "Do you think Santa has come yet?"

In their big fuzzy socks and their oversized bathrobes, Molly and Max crept down the stairs. They stopped halfway down and gasped with delight. Mountains of shiny, colorful presents surrounded the Christmas tree! And the sugar cookies, the milk, and even the little withered carrot were all gone.

"He came!" Max cried.

"And so did the reindeer," observed Molly.

Suddenly, a CRASHING sound in the kitchen echoed loudly down the hallway. Molly and Max both froze. Max looked at Molly and asked nervously, "Do you think Santa is still here?"

Molly grabbed her brother's hand, and together they tip-toed toward the kitchen. As they moved closer, the CRASHING sounds seemed to grow louder and louder. Quietly peering through the kitchen door, Molly let out a gasp.

There—its white tail wiggling happily—was the rump of a reindeer poking out from the fridge!

The kitchen floor, however, was an utter disaster. Food and Tupperware containers were sprawled across the linoleum tile, their contents half-eaten or smushed into goopy hoof-shaped prints. Puddles of milk and soda dribbled down the refrigerator shelves, continuing in long, sticky rivers along the floor.

The pantry had been cleaned out, too—smashed bags of chips and crackers lay busted on the ground. Dented cans of peas and green beans rolled around between crushed boxes of macaroni noodles.

"Nooooo!" wailed Molly and Max in unison, their Christmas merriment suddenly turning to shock and horror.

Their cry of despair startled the reindeer, whose rump twitched and rose up as it dislodged its head from inside the fridge and turned to face them. Chocolate pudding dripped from its antlers. An olive was stuffed up one nostril. And it was licking its lips—which were covered in red Jell-O bits.

Around its neck was a red and green collar adorned with tiny bells. A silver name tag hung from the collar, sparkling in the light of the open fridge.

Jingle

Jingle the reindeer stomped one hoof and shook his head. Chocolate pudding splattered everywhere.

"Looks like he was hungry," observed Max, wiping pudding from his face.

"Hungry or not," Molly declared with a huff, "We've got to get him out of here before Mom and Dad get up."

The children shooed Jingle out of the kitchen and began to scrub and mop, sweep and tidy—salvaging all they could of Mom's big Christmas lunch. Of course the moment they'd finished in the kitchen, they had to start on the dining room... and then the living room... for every room Jingle entered, he sniffed, stomped, and chewed everything within his reach.

Alas, Molly and Max spent most of Christmas Day cleaning up after Jingle and trying to hide him from their parents. They put him outside in the back yard for a bit, but within minutes, he began bellowing and crying, so they had to carefully usher him upstairs to their bedrooms. They decided to make a blanket fort in Max's room where Jingle could sleep. That night, as Jingle snored loudly in the fort beside Max's bed, Molly and Max sat down to write a letter to Santa.

Dear Santa,

Thank you for the gifts. We love them so much! However, is it possible you lost a reindeer last night? Because we found one in our kitchen this morning. His name is Jingle.

Please, if you could come and pick him up at your earliest convenience?

Love,
Molly & Max

Throughout their whole Christmas break, Molly and Max worked hard to take care of Jingle. It hadn't taken long for Mom and Dad to discover the giant reindeer living in the children's bedrooms, but they said he could stay until Santa came for him, as long as Molly and Max were responsible and took good care of him.

They also had to keep him out of the kitchen and from destroying any more of their home.

The children used their Christmas money to buy bags of carrots and oats from the local store. They nearly froze themselves on ten-mile walks so they could keep Jingle in shape. They played every reindeer game they could think of—just to be sure he wouldn't go sneaking into Mister Lemony's crabapple patch to finish off what he'd already started.

And wherever Molly and Max went, Jingle had to come along. When they went out sledding, Jingle was there. On their first go down the hill, Jingle raced after them... and accidentally popped their snow tube with one of his antlers.

When they built a snowman, Jingle tried to help... but couldn't resist a nibble of the carrot nose, or the delicious raisin eyes.

And every night as Jingle snored in the blanket fort, which they were now taking turns having in each of their rooms, Molly and Max wrote letters to Santa.

Dear Santa,

It's Molly and Max again. We hope you and Mrs. Claus and all of the elves and reindeer are doing well! Speaking of reindeer, you might have forgotten that there is one still at our house from Christmas Eve. His name is Jingle. Do you think you could pick him up soon?

Love,
Molly & Max

But Christmas break soon came to an end, and Santa Claus did not come.

Every morning, Jingle followed Molly and Max to school. At lunchtime, he could be found hiding behind the big slide on the playground to gobble up the peanut butter sandwiches and carrot sticks from their lunch boxes. And every afternoon, as Molly and Max marched home with rumbling tummies, Jingle followed merrily along.

In the evenings as they worked on their homework, Jingle couldn't resist trying to help with a nibble here and a chew there. Unfortunately, the excuse, "A reindeer ate my homework," grew very old very quickly with their very doubtful teachers.

Every night, Jingle snuggled up in the blanket fort and began his rackety reindeer snores 'til dawn. And with flashlights in their hands and cotton in their ears, Molly and Max spent sleepless nights writing letter... after letter... after letter.

Dear Santa,

Molly and Max here. We don't know if you remember, but you left a reindeer behind at our house. His name is Jingle. He is a very nice reindeer, but he eats a lot and he poops a lot and he snores all night long. Do you think you can stop by to get him soon?

Love,
Molly & Max

———

The months and the seasons passed, but Santa Claus did not come.

In the summer, Jingle accidentally popped all the floaty tubes in the pool with his antlers. He slurped up all the ice pops before they could even become completely frozen. And he licked off all the sunscreen he could find on Molly or Max (apparently reindeer love the taste of sunscreen.)

In the fall, Jingle jumped in every leaf pile that Molly and Max raked up. He gobbled up their jack-o-lanterns and chewed on every last piece of candy from their trick-or-treat bags. They didn't even get a single bite of Mom's pumpkin pies, because Jingle ate them right off the cooling racks.

When Christmas finally came around again, Molly and Max were ready.

This time, next to the icy-cold milk and the red and green sugar cookies, they left an extra-large plate heaped high with fat, juicy carrots.

And when Jingle tried to follow them up the stairs to bed, Molly and Max shook their heads firmly. "Not tonight, Jingle," they said, and pointed to the plate of carrots.

Before the sun was even up, Max was out of bed and poking at Molly. "Pssst!" he said to his sister, "Do you think Santa came yet?"

In their big fuzzy socks and their oversized bathrobes, the siblings crept down the stairs to peek. The sugar cookies and milk were gone. The fat, juicy carrots were gone, too! They checked all around the mountains of shiny presents. They searched the dining room and the kitchen. They peeked out into the yard—just in case. But Jingle the reindeer was gone.

That Christmas, Max and Molly could do anything they wanted. They played with all their new toys but didn't have to include any silly reindeer games. They went sledding on their new snow tubes (which did not pop). They built the best and biggest snowman ever (that wasn't missing its raisin eyes or carrot nose.) They stuffed themselves full with all the Christmas treats they wanted (even though they got little tummy aches as a result.)

When they went to bed that night, they both lay awake listening to the peace and quiet, with no snoring reindeer. (Although, suddenly it felt a little too quiet.)

They both threw off their blankets, and Molly ran into Max's room, where they built one last fort beside Max's bed. Cuddling up together in the fort, Molly and Max wrote one last letter to Santa.

Dear Santa,

Thank you so much for all of the presents. We had a really fun day playing with the toys and eating lots of treats. But that's not why we're writing. We want to know if you could please send Jingle our love. And if he ever wants to stop by to eat—or play—or stay for just a little bit—we'd be very happy to see him.

Love,
Molly & Max

P.S.: And we promise to leave him lots and lots of carrots next year!

10

THE SANTA S

Willow had been staring at the snowfall outside for so long that a little shelf of snow had built up on the outside of the window ledge. Mrs. Abury's monotonous voice had done nothing to drag her out of her daydream, nor had her stupendously boring lesson on decimal places and fractions.

It seemed she wasn't the only one who had tuned out. Her classmates were restless for the recess bell, because the fresh powdered snow was calling for them to start an epic snowball fight, create a snow family or build an igloo (which last year had provided the added bonus of collapsing on top of Kyle Bouchard, who had feigned frostbite to get the afternoon off. His dramatic mother had then marched him to the emergency room and convinced the doctor to write a note to keep him out of school for the remainder of the Christmas term). A lot of kids had sighed with relief at this news. Kyle wasn't exactly the nicest kid. In fact, he was a huge jerk.

Willow turned in her seat to see what Kyle was doing, other than ignoring Mrs. Abury. As she'd guessed, he was sniggering and leaning over his desk, trying his hardest to ruin someone's day. That someone was Holly Bell and her enormous mass of curls was Kyle's target, as he carefully and quietly inserted pencils, one by one, into her hair. Three already stuck out at wonky angles, and he was concentrating hard on adding a fourth, biting his bottom lip to keep himself from laughing as kids around him watched with amused expressions. Willow returned her gaze to the window, feeling uncomfortable about not doing anything.

People were always picking on Holly. She had only been at the school for a few months, but rumor had it she'd been at her last school for the same short amount of time, and the school before that, too. Sour-faced Frankie Davis told everyone her family was poor and went dumpster-diving on weekends. Dylan Dawson said her parents were criminals and were on the run from the police. Kelsie Abraham was convinced she was a witch who practiced voodoo, because she was always scribbling things down in a notebook, and people saw her talking to birds. Kelsie was certain she was casting spells.

All Willow knew was that Holly kept to herself, and it seemed to be with good reason. Despite the tales about her parents, Willow doubted that Holly even had any. She'd never seen anyone meet her at the school gates, and no one had come for her to the parent-teacher conference last month. Willow understood loneliness, ever since her best friend Claire had moved to Washington last year. She hadn't really found anyone else to hang out with since, and although she and Claire spoke all the time on the phone, it just wasn't the same.

The bell rang, ending the school day, and jolted Willow out of her thoughts. Chairs scraped back and papers scattered. As Holly stood, the pencils fell from her hair and clattered all over the floor. Kyle and some other kids howled with laughter and pushed past her, heading for the door so quickly that Mrs. Abury couldn't summon the energy to scold him before he was gone. The class filed out and headed for the main doors.

When Willow stepped outside, the cold air brushed her cheeks. She watched Holly walk down the path as snowballs began to soar over her head. Her pace was fast, but not fast enough to avoid the snowball that arched like an arrow and landed on her shoulder. The celebration from a nearby group of boys suggested

Dylan Dawson was the culprit. Willow sighed and shook her head. She made her way down the path after Holly. She didn't know what she intended to say, but she needed to know if she was alright.

After turning right out of school and heading down the slushy road, Willow found her courage ebbing away, and fell into step a few feet behind Holly. The only sound was their trudging feet, and Willow suddenly worried that she appeared to be Holly's next tormentor.

"Hey!" she called. The sound of her own voice gave her a fright!

Holly turned around. "Are you following me?" she asked.

"Um, not really, I... just wanted to check you were okay," Willow mumbled, closing the gap between them. She looked at Holly's pretty earrings peeking out from underneath her hair. They were round and ruby-red, like little berries. Holly smiled shyly.

"Thanks, that's sweet of you. Yeah, I'm okay. It's nothing I can't handle," she said.

"Do you live much further? I can walk you home, if you want," Willow offered. She was trying hard to push aside the whispers of the other kids, but she was secretly curious about where Holly actually lived.

"Sure, it's only a couple more blocks. Atnas Road – do you know it?"

Willow did know it. She furrowed her brow in confusion. Atnas Road was, as far as she knew, lined with abandoned or derelict houses from a flood a few years back. It was at the bottom of a hill, and not far from the river bank, making it a magnet for a natural disaster. The girls continued their walk, Willow deep in thought, and Holly looking up into the sky, watching the birds flit past. She held her left earlobe absent-mindedly.

"Are you looking forward to Christmas?" Holly asked, tucking her hands into her pockets.

Willow shrugged. "I guess so. My mom is big on decorating. She's been doing it for *weeks*. I can barely make it to the staircase without falling over something. We keep losing our dog in the tinsel," she joked. "How about you?"

"I don't really do much for Christmas. Have you asked for any nice gifts?" asked Holly.

Willow pondered for a while. "Wellllll, I could do with a new bike. My old one is a bit scratched up. Or a new diary. Those kinds of things."

Holly's laugh tinkled beautifully, like bells. "You don't sound too sure about those. Are you sure they're what you want?" she grinned. She stopped in front of a house with an untidy front garden, a weathered porch, and flecked paint pockmarking the wooden exterior. Apart from the snow, there wasn't anything remotely festive about it – no Christmas lights, or yard decorations, or even a tree peeping out from the living room window. It was the saddest house Willow had ever seen.

"This is me. It was nice talking to you, Willow. Thanks for walking me home. See you in school tomorrow?" asked Holly.

Willow smiled and nodded. "Sure, see you then."

And with that, Holly walked up the path and disappeared through the creaking front door. Willow was mystified. She turned and walked home, promising herself that she would be extra kind to Holly from that moment forward.

Over the next two weeks, Willow and Holly spoke every day. They hung out at recess and sat together at lunch. They paired up in classes and walked each other home. At first, Willow feared she'd become a target of Kyle and his cronies, but she and Holly soon worked out how to avoid or outsmart them. It was the first time Willow had felt truly happy since Claire had left, and she soon stopped noticing Holly's strange little habits. She did seem to scrawl in a notepad wherever she went, but never shared what she was writing. She often bumped into people or tripped because her head was craned to the sky as she watched various birds.

On the day before Christmas break, Willow and Holly walked out the main doors together. All the kids flooded out of the building, cheering in celebration of the Christmas break. Willow pulled her coat tightly around her. It was icily cold, with more snow due that night. Holly was holding her coat and started to put it on when, like a flash, Kyle Bouchard tore past them, yanking Holly's coat out of her hands as he went.

"Think fast, freak!" he yelled, sprinting toward the road. Holly and Willow, along with a few of their classmates, looked on in horror as Kyle spun his arm like a wind-mill and launched the coat up a lamppost. It swung over the curved bar and wrapped around the metal, leaving it suspended far above their heads. Kyle guffawed with delight. He could hardly believe he'd managed such an awesome throw.

"Good luck with that, Jolly Holly!" he shouted, before running home. They chased after him but stopped at the lamppost, where Holly sighed and sat under a nearby tree, eyes trained on her coat. Willow gazed up at it, anger building deep inside. It simply wasn't fair.

What did Holly ever do to deserve to be bullied so horribly?

"Come on, Holly. We'll never get it down from there. Let's go home. I'll get my dad to bring a ladder tomorrow morning to get it down," Willow said.

Holly shook her head and rested her chin in her hand. "Nah, don't worry, we'll be able to get it. C'mon, sit down next to me, it won't be long. We just have to wait until everyone's gone."

Willow was bewildered. The lamppost was taller than both of them stacked on top of each other. She couldn't imagine how they'd get it down without a very tall ladder. But she settled down next to Holly, who had started to shiver, and waited until the kids and cars disappeared off to their warm, cozy homes. Soon, there was no one around.

"Now," said Holly, "let's call for some help from a friend."

Suddenly, a small bird flew over to the lamppost, flapping its wings to stay in place beside the coat. Willow watched in utter amazement as the bird used its beak to nudge at the sleeves. It looked like it was trying to loosen it! Just then, another bird appeared, and another, and all three pecked and beat their wings until the coat slid from the lamppost and dropped to the ground in a heap. Willow was so stunned she stayed frozen in place as Holly stood up and casually walked over to collect it.

"What the..." Willow gasped, as Holly flashed her a smile.

"Wanna see what other tricks I have up my sleeve?" she asked with a grin before she began running home. Her words were like a firework up Willow's butt. She scrambled to her feet and chased after Holly as they ran toward Holly's house. When they arrived, breathless, in front of her home on Atnas Road, Willow could hardly believe she was finally going to see the inside of the mysterious house. Holly turned the key in the lock and opened the front door, ushering Willow in behind her.

The downstairs of the house was surprisingly neat and tidy. Nothing looked as worn as the outside of the house, and the staircase was carpeted in a rich, red hue. Holly jogged straight up the stairs, with Willow on her heels. As she neared the top, she heard a faint whirring sound. Willow followed Holly toward a closed door at the back of the house. Holly jingled her keychain to find the correct key to unlock it. Willow held her breath.

Holly pushed the door open with a flourish and stepped inside. Willow gasped at what she saw. Computer screens and monitors covered every wall. They seemed to be filming areas around the town – the school's playground, the local movie theater, a restaurant and a nearby grocery store. A huge desk was filled with all sorts of electrical equipment, gadgets and notepads. Binoculars and cameras on straps hung from the ceiling. Jars of glowing lights lined shelves above a messy bed in a corner. A box of elf dolls was overflowing at the foot of the bed.

"What… what is all this?" Willow whispered.

"Ah, it's all part of the job. I do always try to be tidy, but things can get… out of control when I'm on a mission. And this town has been my biggest mission yet."

"A… mission?" Willow asked, picking up a small webcam disguised as a Christmas bauble. A little red light glowed within. She quickly set it down again.

"Well, you know when you're a little kid, and your parents tell you to be good so you aren't put on the naughty list? Well… guess who's listening," Holly said proudly, even adding a little bow when she'd finished.

"You're a… spy?"

"Sure am! My official title is a junior Santa Spy, but with the amount of work I do, I should definitely get promoted soon," she squealed. "People think Santa has this big old book with hundreds of thousands of names in it. But technology these days has made it so much easier to keep track of everyone. It's all on our Santa system. See my earrings? They record sound. It's easier to play back conversations when I get home so I can be absolutely sure who's naughty and who's nice. And these... are my favorites!"

Holly went to the window and pulled it open. A moment later, a small robin arrived and perched on the sill, staring at Willow intently.

"These are my robin-bots. They fly around town, capturing conversations from all the kids." Willow edged forward to see the bird a little closer. It looked so real; she couldn't believe it was robotic. Holly held out her finger, and the bird hopped onto it. She carried it over to the computers, and set it on a pad, which began to glow.

"There you go. It's uploading. I should be able to fit the last few kids onto the database by tonight. What do you think? Neat, huh?"

"It's incredible," Willow breathed, letting the sights before her sink in. She couldn't believe Holly worked for Santa. THE Santa!

"As you can imagine, there are some kids who really *are* on the naughty list," Holly chuckled and winked at Willow, before crouching down and opening a mini fridge below the desk. She pulled out some freshly baked, warm cookies. From a *fridge?!*

"Holly, you've got to tell me more!" Willow exclaimed, as she took a seat and gazed at the screens.

Willow was sad when Holly told her she had to leave on Christmas Eve. She'd worked hard over the Christmas season, and now had to return to her headquarters for some rest before work started up again. They'd hugged tightly at the top of Atnas Road, and Willow had asked if she'd ever see her again.

"I don't see why not. My job takes me all over, but can be pretty lonely; it's good to know I have a friend somewhere in the world. I want you to know that I'll never forget your kindness, and you will always have a place on the nice list. I promise!" Holly laughed. "And trust me… you'll get exactly what you want for Christmas."

Willow smiled sadly as she parted with her new friend. She trudged home and was cheered up by her mom's crazy light show on their front yard. She walked past the sparkling reindeer and the singing snowman to the front door, adorned with a wreath that was bigger than a bus tire.

Opening the door, she could have sworn she heard a familiar giggle from her living room. She gasped as a face she knew and loved appeared in the doorway. The very best Christmas present of all, and one that Holly knew was at the top of her wish list.

"CLAIRE!"

11

THE LITTLEST CHRISTMAS TREE

It was December at last, and the Christmas tree farm was teeming with happy families. They came bubbling with Christmas cheer, ready to find the very best tree to decorate with shimmery bulbs and strings of blinking, colorful lights. They came with the hope that the most perfect tree in the world was waiting for them right here. And every Christmas tree on the Christmas tree farm stood up tall, waiting and hoping to be noticed.

The children, all bundled up in puffy jackets, tall winter boots and thick mittens, went tromping and romping through the new-fallen snow. They romped from tree to tree, hunting and hallooing to their moms and dads whenever they'd found a tree that looked good.

"Look at that one!" one would cry.

"This one is *perfect!*" another would exclaim.

"And the one over here smells the *piniest* of all!" several others would claim.

Their moms and dads would come along to scrutinize their choices. "This one is so straight and tall," one dad would admire.

"That one has the bushiest needles I've ever seen," a mom would observe.

"The one over there is the most beautiful shade of green I've seen," still another mother would say.

One by one, the trees on the Christmas tree farm were chosen by joyful children and hauled away by contented moms and dads. Sadly, not every Christmas tree finds a home right away. Some trees take longer to be noticed than others, and some wait many Decembers to find their perfect homes.

So, the trees that were not chosen on the first day did not sigh in despair. They simply fluffed up their bushy green needles, stretched themselves ever-so-slightly taller, and waited for the next day. When new families arrived glowing with Christmas cheer, more lucky trees were caressed by joyful children and hauled away by contented moms and dads.

Now, not every tree found a family on the next day, either. The Christmas tree farm was very large, and there were many lovely trees to choose from. Yet it could be said that the further up the tree farm hill, the fewer children hunted and hallooed—and the fewer moms and dads were willing to haul a tree back down.

The trees up the hill grew burlier, patchier, and more and more crooked; these were the trees that were not so very liked. These were the trees with bare spots here and there that could not simply be covered up with a Christmas bulb or a string of twinkling lights. These were the trees with uneven branches or misshapen trunks—the shapes you didn't find in holiday scenes or Christmas picture books.

And in the farthest place, up, up atop the tree farm hill behind the burliest, patchiest, and most crookedest of Christmas trees, grew one little pine tree. The little pine was so far back and so very well hidden that it wasn't even noticed on the first day... or the second... or even the third. Alas, it wasn't the kind of tree that would be noticed most days.

You see, the little pine tree was very little indeed. While its sapling brothers and sisters had shot up to great heights, the little pine had chugged along at half their speed. While the other trees stood with solid branches and bushy, green needles, the little pine had many mostly-bare branches and very little green color to speak of. In fact, many of its needles were yellowish and brown; even the bark on its branches was rough and uneven.

And to top it all off, the little pine was quite crooked all the way to its very tip—not at all a nice cap for crowning with a Christmas star.

Being so far back and so very behind, the little pine tended not to get any people-visitors... though it did get quite a few visitors of another kind. Gray squirrels and wood mice came to nibble on snacks from its little seed cones. Cottontail rabbits rustled beneath its needly skirts, and all sorts of birds took turns napping on its mostly-bare branches. Even the red fox and the brown deer passed by now and then to scratch their itching ears on its rough, uneven bark.

But these were not the kind of visitors that the little pine had imagined and hoped for. Since its days as a mere sapling only inches from the ground (so many Decembers ago), the little pine had dreamed of ornaments and shiny bulbs, of strings of things in every shimmery Christmas color. It had dreamed of bringing holiday cheer to a loving family who would happily deck its strong branches, its tall, straight trunk, and its bushy green needles with hundreds of beautiful ornaments.

However, the little pine tree did not have strong branches. It did not grow a tall, straight trunk, or bushy green needles. And so, while all the other Christmas trees were plucked up merrily from the lot, the little pine stood far up and back, waiting beneath the shadows of the burliest, patchiest, and most crookedest of trees.

Day after day it waited. And as the farm gate shut at the end of each day, it told itself that tomorrow would be different.

Even in the very last days before Christmas, the little pine tree heard the clomping of snow boots tromping up, up, the hill. It shook out its needles to make them as bushy as possible, and it stretched up, up just as tall as it could. The rabbits in its skirts rustled away and the birds in its branches took flight. The squirrels and mice twittered as they skittered down and out.

And then, bursting through the burliest, patchiest, and most crookedest of the trees came two children: a little boy out of breath, quickly followed by his big sister.

"Look at this one!" the little brother cried. He rushed up to the little pine and brushed along its branches with his mittens, smiling.

But his big sister took one look up and down the tree—and sniffed judgmentally. "Not that one," she scowled.

"It's got a crooked top! There's a big empty spot on one side and its needles are too yellow. Its branches are too skinny. And," she finished with a long frown drawing down her mouth, "it's much too small to be a real Christmas tree."

She turned on the heel of her boot. "These over here are much taller," she said, waving a mittened hand up towards the burliest, patchiest, and most crookedest of the trees.

And the little pine watched as the children hallooed for their mom and dad, who came up, up the hill to haul away one of the burly trees.

One by one, even all of these trees found a home. And when Christmas Eve came, the little pine looked down and around from atop the tree farm hill. A blanket of white snow covered the lot—and not a single tree was left except the little pine itself.

That day, not another child hunted or hallooed—not another mom or dad inspected or hauled. Every family was busy at home, each with their perfect Christmas tree all decked with shimmery bulbs and strings of blinking, colorful lights.

To the very last minute, the little pine remained hopeful. It shook out its needles to make them as bushy as possible, and it stretched up, up just as tall as it could. But no one came that day, and as the evening set in, the tree farm gate shut up tight. There atop the barren hill, the little pine stood all alone—its branches full of nibbling squirrels and napping birds, and its needly skirts tickled by wild rabbit whiskers.

If a tree could cry, the little pine tree would have done just that. Instead, it sank deep into its crooked form. It let go of its last fluffy needles. And it fell into a cold and lonely sleep.

Some Christmas trees take longer to be noticed than others, and some wait many Decembers to find their homes. But what the little pine tree did not realize is that it had been noticed all along, just not by those it expected.

In the darkening eve before Christmas Day, the animals of the wood came out. With whispers and rustles and silent swoops, they set to work on the little pine tree.

The gray squirrels and the wood mice wove long, festive garlands of acorn tops and little holly berries.

The sparrows and the chickadees plucked small crabapples from the wild apple trees and carried them, one by one, in their beaks to hang on the branches.

The cottontail rabbits pulled up long, green grasses to fill in empty patches.

With its soft, fluffy tail, the red fox brushed away any dirt and dust to make every needle shine.

And the brown deer stretched up to the crooked tree top where it gently placed one perfect poinsettia star.

As the Christmas morning sun reached out to warm the hilltop, the little pine woke. The gray squirrels, the wood mice, the rabbits and the birds, the red fox and the brown deer all gathered 'round.

For a moment, the little pine seemed confused—until at last the light of morning touched its new Christmas coat. It was an extraordinary sight; a Christmas tree like no other!

It stood up tall and bright, adorned with strings of colorful things—the work of those who had always noticed it; the work of those to whom it gave shelter and food and a place to rest for so many Decembers.

As the morning passed, people walking by enjoyed a wonderful Christmas treat. They called to their neighbors and tromped up, up the hill by the dozen. Soon, the tree farm was teeming with jolly Christmas cheer—and the little pine stood at the center of it all!

It is true that some trees take longer to be noticed than others, and some wait for many Decembers to find their perfect homes. But the little pine was already home—and for many Decembers to come, it would be loved and adorned by those who had always noticed it.

12

THE REINDEER DIARIES

So, the Big Man has asked me to write out a diary entry for a night in the life of one of his reindeer. Some radio station in the South Pole wanted to spice up their Sunday evening show, and he picked me because he thought out of the nine of us, I'd be the best deer for the job. I mean, other than the hoof complication—I've hired a wonderful, kind, talented elf named Tinsel to do the whole writing bit.

"Did you just add something else in?"

"No, Dasher, I didn't."

"It looked like you were writing some extra words before 'elf' just now..."

"Not at all. I promise it's just your long eyelashes confusing you, my furry friend."

Anyway, I guess the radio listeners are dying to know what we get up to on Christmas Eve. And I get it. Everyone has vacation fever, and my clan and I cover some serious miles in a single night. Sure, we don't exactly get to catch a tan (though many a joke was made back in the day about Dolphy's nose being the result of some savage sunburn) but in terms of the aerial views... there's nothing quite like it.

The night isn't without its difficulties though. Don't for a second think we have it easy! It's heavy and hungry work, and depending on who draws the short carrot, you might end up with your nose behind Donner's backside (and that stench is enough to knock you out for at least two continents). We usually start out with a big meal, while those amazing, jolly little folk—

"Are you going off-script again, elf?"

"No Dasher, I'm simply writing with a flourish. It's all complimentary to you, of course."

—load up the sleigh. We usually get a barrel each of the good stuff—moss and herbs and grass and leaves... I'm slobbering at the thought of it! It's all the very best quality, as you can imagine. We're professionals in the paddock. We train all year for that one night, so some good grub is absolutely essential. We wash it all down with some water from the bubbling streams of the Arctic—a refreshing beverage for only the best

animals around. Trust me, lions might be kings of the jungle, but reindeer are the princes of the Pole.

"Actually, let's scratch that, Tinsel. The polar bears might listen to this show."

We also like to eat the odd mushroom to really get us into the festive spirit. However, Prancer, Vixen, Comet, Cupid, Blitzen, Rudolph and I are usually in cahoots when it comes to this because those feisty fungi really do wreak havoc on Donner's digestive tract. Just one of those delicious toadstools sends his rear end into some sort of operatic performance of flatulence, and it really ruins the mood when you're flying 311 million miles around the blasted planet to the sound of ferocious farting.

Luckily, old Donner isn't the brightest bell in the jingle stick. We can usually convince him he's eaten so quickly that he simply didn't notice he'd scarfed up his mushroom at the bottom of his barrel. Then we play Rock, Parchment, Clippers to decide who should get his share. Vixen has won two years in a row now. Between you and me, I'm pretty sure he's cheating.

After our meal of dreams, it's time to get hooked up to the old sleigh. Obviously, Dolphy never has to get involved with the squabbling over places – he just sashays up to the front with that glowing hooter of his and lets the elves strap him in. Comet usually prefers to be beside Cupid so they can discuss snow hockey tactics. Comet somehow managed to become a referee for the Winter Wanderers elfin team a few years back, which he takes very seriously, and never seems to notice that his presence on the pitch causes considerable chaos because his hooves don't gel with ice skates. One brave elf once jeered that Bambi should have been a good example for deer on ice, but an antler to his posterior caused him to take flight and land about a mile away in a snow drift.

"Buddy is still an inch shorter to this day because of that unfortunate incident!"

"Oh shush, Tinsel, this isn't about you. He should have known better than to mock the moose."

Vixen is a good companion to be next to for the ride. She often tells hilarious stories about her cousin, an elk who lives in the Rocky Mountains. Or, although he's a dope, it can be a good idea to try and muscle in beside Donner instead of being behind him—because, you know, of the backside belching.

When everyone is strapped in, the Big Man arrives and we can't help but become a trifle overeager. You could call it fawning, I suppose. Terribly embarrassing, but although we've done the trip a thousand times, we still feel the little thrill in our bellies when we see that enormous red velvet coat and hear that booming voice.

He clambers into the sleigh and bellows that deep Ho, Ho, Ho,
and we hear those ~~tiny silly creatures~~ astonishing, magnifi-
cent, magical folk—

"Tinsel, this is MY DIARY!"

— manically clapping their hands from inside the workshop
at the sight of the enormous sack, bulging with the gifts they
have worked on all year. It takes about five of them on each
side of the barn doors to pull them open, and we get the first
taste of crisp, cold air. It's our rocket fuel. Our double shot of
espresso. The sweetest sugar donut. When that magical air
fills our lungs, our hooves start to dance and prance (Prancer
practically breaks into the Lindy Hop, naturally) and we
lunge against our reins with excitement. But nobody moves
until Santa salutes the elves and pulls on his gloves. We
strain our ears, waiting for the call, so we can take off in a
majestic gallop. He clears his throat and finally snaps the
reins.

"ONWARDS!" he booms, the hundreds of bells adorning our
straps and halters filling the night air with tinkling and
jangling. Our hooves begin to thunder as we lurch forward—
and we always seem to forget just how heavy the dang sleigh
is. When we're airborne, of course, our magic makes it as
light as a feather, but take-off is always a test of our brute
strength (which we have in abundance, obviously).

As we gain speed into the night, and we find each other's rhythm, we sense the right time to lift from the snow and feel the wind pick up underneath our hooves. I'll never admit it to him, but that red nose of Rudolph's really is a brilliantly bulbous beacon to guide us. When we settle into a level formation again, we relax and almost go into auto-deer—our cycling legs never wane or tire, and we can enjoy counting the stars (or discussing defense positions, or listening to funny stories, depending on your partner).

When we arrive at our first house, it's all a matter of one, skill; and two, patience. We avoid eating carrots throughout the rest of the year, so we can savor every last one left for us beside a fireplace. It's to be expected that your turn for a tasty treat comes only every ninth house – and this is sometimes even less often if the occupants forget that there are large, hairy beasts doing all the hard work on the roof, and the big old fellow simply sits in the sleigh ~~and occasionally takes a nap~~

"You will not slander Santa's good name! I'm removing that bit—"

"Tinsel, this is an uncensored diary entry. The listeners will want full insight into Christmas night..."

"It's just your shameless plug for more carrots, you stinking beast!"

"I knew I should have hired Gumdrop for this gig..."

"YOU'RE NOT EVEN PAYING ME!"

A N Y W A Y, we reindeer are always so grateful for the delicious treats left by the boys and girls of the world. It certainly does perk us up as we fly from city to city. We have had a few... mishaps over the years (Blitzen tells the best story about when Santa lost a boot in a roaring fire. The Big Man finished off the rest of England hobbling around with a soaking sock on his left foot).

One year we forgot the naughty list and it was, quite frankly, bedlam. Some badly behaved folk got gifts they most definitely did not deserve, and Santa only noticed after he had delivered three Barbie dolls and a toy train to prisoners in Alcatraz (I would like it noted that they ALSO did not leave us any carrots).

When the sack is finally empty, and the sleigh feels impossibly light, we kick off our worn-out hooves one last time and head back to the North Pole. Mrs. Claus always switches on our heated blankets before we arrive home, which is simply delightful—and she usually leaves Santa to snooze in the sleigh until those mince pies begin to digest.

There you have it, a night in the life of me, the dashing Dasher.

"Wasn't that a splendid bonding exercise, Tinsel? I actually think you make a fine writer indeed. I could make this journaling a hobby! Let's do this again next week."

"Over my cooked sugarplums!"

Ah well, another day, another sleigh!

Made in United States
Orlando, FL
05 December 2023